THRESHOLD

John Nelson

Other Books by John Nelson

Starborn

Transformations

Matrix of the Gods

Solstice Shift

The Magic Mirror

I, Human

A Guide to Energetic Healing

New Mexican Standoff

This Moment Paradise

The Serpent of Time

The Miracle of Anna

The Singularity of Consciousness

THRESHOLD

A Crisis Ignites
a Universal
Awakening

JOHN NELSON

BOOKWORKS PUBLISHING

First published by Bookworks Publishing, 2022

Bookworks Publishing Company
P.O. Box 1085
Kihei, HI 96753
www.johnnelsonbookworks.com

e-book edition published in March 2022

ISBN: 978-0-578-27844-5

Cover and interior design by Frame25 Productions
Cover photograph © Kjpargeter c/o Shutterstock.com

For the brave and heroic people of Ukraine,
who are not only fighting for their freedom
but for the soul of humanity.

Author's Note

I began writing this novel—or downloading it would be more appropriate since it came to me almost fully formed—in the first week of December 2021. At the time, no one figured that Russia would invade Ukraine and devastate it. What I envision here is a possible global awakening of humanity to our oneness not only as citizens of separate countries but also as the one Soul of Humanity, which has been stirred, I believe, by our worldwide response to this tragedy. I can only hope that from such a crisis, this one or others to come, we will finally awaken to what the poet John Donne said centuries ago as more than lofty sentiment:

No man is an island,
Entire of itself.
Each is a piece of the continent,
A part of the main.
If a clod be washed away by the sea,
Europe [the world] is the less.
As well as if a promontory were.
As well as if a manor of thine own
Or of thine friends were.
Each man's death diminishes me,
For I am involved in mankind.
Therefore, send not to know
For whom the bell tolls,
It tolls for thee.

Acknowledgments

I want to thank two of my longtime friends and authors, Donald Altman and Frank DeMarco, who read the first draft of this novel and pointed out its many deficiencies in terms of fleshing it out. I did add many of their suggestions, but this is speculative fiction, driven more by its ideas than by its characters, and I'll rest my case there.

1

San Francisco, California

For Jungian analyst Dr. Maria Amidala, it started with an analysand's claim of a "waking dream," or as the psychiatrist termed it. Sitting in her office in a four-story brownstone building overlooking the Bay, with sunrays slanting through wooden blinds, dust motes twirling in the air, she first thought of Carl Jung's use of active imagination. During his inner self-exploration, a "confrontation with the unconscious," this eminent psychologist would isolate characters from his dreams or unconscious upsurges and conduct an imaginative conversation with them to understand what they represented. Some called these waking dreams. The absorption of this archetypal energy helped cure him of his latent psychosis, as he freely admitted.

Maria had used this technique with some of her long-term analysands, but that was not the case here, as the very serious Catherine Dumont adamantly insisted, shaking her head. It happened outside of herself in the real world, and she had no such verbal interaction with the "viewees," as she characterized them. This gave Maria pause. At least the young woman, like some of her analysands, didn't facetiously ask if she was related to Padmé Amidala from the *Star War* movies. To which she would reply, "No, it's Italian for beautiful flower, and the surname goes back to the Middle

Ages." What would go unmentioned at such times was her name's association with the limbic system's amygdala, which processes fear responses, or how it is generally characterized—a simplification of its broader function.

Maria had lost her parents in a car accident at age ten, one which she barely survived. This tragedy led to fear-based emotional problems and the use of prescription drugs by a stream of psychologists/psychiatrists brought in by her mother's sister, Aunt Dorothy, to "deal with it." It wasn't until one of them, noting her violent dreams, had recommended a Jungian therapist for further exploration that Maria found an opening to a greater sense of self. By then a dismissive teenager, she had asked Dr. Paul Hall, "And what drugs are you going to put me on?"

"My dear, I don't prescribe drugs, or rarely; I conduct psychodynamic therapy."

This clarification intrigued her, and she went along with his therapeutic approach emphasizing natural tendencies as the keystone to growth. But it wasn't until he told her at one point, "You are not your feelings or your thoughts nor who you think you are, but so much more," that the light of true awareness dawned. Precocious and highly intellectual, Maria started reading about Carl Jung and his psychology, beginning with *Memories, Dreams, and Reflections*. But it was reading Marie-Louise von Franz's *Shadow and Evil in Fairy Tales* that set her course. This book explained why evil things happen and their symbolic meaning, and more than anything else, it helped her deal with the loss of her parents.

She received her undergraduate, master's, and doctorate degrees in psychotherapy from Stanford and had gone there because of its emphasis on psychology rather than the curative use of pharmacology. She became certified as a Jungian analyst with coursework in

England and Switzerland. Unfortunately, by the time Maria arrived in Zurich, von Franz had long since retired and was too reclusive to receive curious admirers. However, she did attend the memorial service for her in 1998.

Maria leaned forward. Her long brown hair fell over her forehead, and she had to brush a few strands aside. She asked Catherine, "And why do you call these episodes dreams, not just psychic impressions?"

"Like dreams, they have somewhat of a narrative flow."

"Interesting. One associated with something happening in your life?"

"They're not compensatory," Catherine insisted.

Maria sat back. *Ah, a smart one. She's done her research.* Most psychologists associated Dr. Jung's dream theory solely with the concept of compensation. The unconscious mind compensates in dreams for an unrealistic conscious attitude and often with an exaggerated and/or opposite situation to bring the psyche into balance. However, no true Jungian would pigeonhole the entirety of Jung's dream theory as such.

The two of them looked at each other for a long moment. Finally, Catherine added, "I tried reading Jung's *Red Book*, but it was too . . . harrowing." Maria waited her out. "Actually, it scared me. I had to put it down."

"Yes, many of my colleagues feel the same way." She paused. "Theory is one thing; chaotic unconscious experience, like Jung's, is entirely different."

Catherine leaned forward and peered into her doctor's eyes. "But not for you, I take it?"

Maria laughed to break the tension. "Yes, I've read the book in its entirety. Some of my colleagues call me 'The Princess of

Darkness.'" She could almost see the Padmé Amidala reference come to Catherine's mind, but the woman dismissed it to her credit. Good. Maybe she was ready for the deep dark work.

"So, shall we get on with it?" Maria asked.

Catherine closed her eyes. "The first so-called waking dream happened three months ago. A woman, someone I didn't recognize at the time, walks into a farmer's market, but not one I've ever seen. She goes from one stall to another, then stops and picks up a large grapefruit. Smells it. Shakes her head and then throws it to the ground, splattering it everywhere." She opened her eyes.

"Did that image scare you?"

"Yes, a little bit. I mean, these waking dreams just pop up in my day-to-day life. I now know how delusional people must feel." Catherine gathered herself. "The funny thing is that the woman looked in my direction or from where I was viewing the scene as if I were physically present. Then she shook her body as if sloughing off something and hurried away."

"And where were you when this happened?"

"I had just driven off the Golden Gate Bridge on my way home from work and had to pull over."

"You drive this route every day?" Maria asked.

"Yes, to and from Mill Valley."

"And all this time, you've never seen a produce truck maybe drop something that splattered on the roadway?"

Catherine shook her head and added impatiently, "No, nor have I ever had that experience in a grocery store. As I said, these waking dreams aren't compensatory."

"And how many other episodes have there been since then?"

"Two more. Both with different people, but nobody I know."

Maria sat back, and then it hit her. "You said 'someone you didn't recognize at the time.'"

"Yes," Catherine replied with excitement, "then I came across her picture or someone who looked like her on Facebook. One of my social-media friends."

Maria had to hold back from saying, "Ah-ha." Instead, she examined this young woman more closely: mid-twenties, short blond hair, sharp nose, inquisitive eyes, athletic. She was wearing a dark professional pantsuit. "And you sent her a message and asked if she had actually had this experience?" *If so, bold of her.*

Catherine vigorously nodded her head. "Yes, and she accused me of spying on her from the next aisle and unfriended me. I mean, she lives halfway across the country, but she wouldn't listen to reason. Also, I got the feeling I saw it happen at the same time. So it wasn't precognitive."

Maria couldn't dismiss that this waking dream was some form of telepathy or even, since the first woman sensed Catherine's presence, maybe an astral projection. Unlike most scientists, she didn't dismiss such possibilities, nor did Jung.

"And the others?"

Catherine closed her eyes and sighed as if anxious to purge herself of them.

AFTER ONE MORE SESSION that afternoon, Maria had her secretary, Claire, make a reservation for her at Scoma's on Fisherman's Wharf. She had tentatively set a date with her sometime boyfriend, Michael Davenport, but bowed out. Maria wanted to be alone but among people and look out over the Bay to allow her subconscious mind to process her session with young Catherine Dumont. Michael wasn't one to follow her into the depths. The woman's recall of her other waking dreams was consistent with the first, although she didn't recognize either of the people, and none of them brought up traumatic memories. But again, she said these viewees looked back in her direction or to her point of view. Maria had the woman schedule another session at the end of the week. She wanted to delve deeper into Catherine's psyche to see what else was happening in her life, her nighttime dreams in particular. Maria needed more personal context to understand these episodes, or that was the recommended procedure. She smiled as if that dictate applied to something so unconventional.

But since the first incident had been verified as an actual occurrence in someone else's life, it possibly brought them out of the realm of the personal unconscious into a more collective or objective unconscious strata. She couldn't help but think of the German patients coming to Carl Jung in the 1920s with an upsurge of foreboding archaic-Germanic shadow images presaging, as he would later understand, the rise of Nazism and Germany's fall into mass psychosis. Was Catherine Dumont experiencing a presage of another collective movement from that realm, and given its relatively benign content, of a positive nature? Maria shook her head. She was getting ahead of herself, even if current world events were unsettling. Either way, such a connection could be foreboding, which accounted for this woman's trepidation.

Maria had noticed how more and more of her analysands were becoming overwhelmed by the complexity of modern life and its almost maniacal pace, that superficial online exchanges were replacing real, human interactions and diminishing our feelings for each other. It was interesting and maybe telling that Dumont's first episode involved a Facebook friend, the media outlet with three-billion monthly users worldwide. This recalled a line from a 1916 essay by Jung where the concept of the "Collective Unconscious" first appeared and that it "encompass[es] the soul of humanity." *A soul,* she thought, *through which everybody is connected. Revelatory indeed.*

At Scoma's, given that Maria was a preferred customer, she was immediately taken to her favorite window table, though they asked to see her vaccination card at that time. Her long gray-knitted skirt swished with her legs moving back and forth. At the table, she looked out the wide window as a white pleasure yacht glided across the bay waters. Maria spotted people at the stern bundled up on this cool evening, sitting back in captain chairs and drinking beers, whiling away the time. Maria tried to remember the last time she had been that carefree but couldn't.

The waiter approached her; she didn't need a menu and ordered the Alaskan Halibut and a glass of Chardonnay, with a tossed salad as an appetizer. He left, and the glass of wine was promptly served. Maria took a sip and looked out the window again. The yacht had passed, revealing the antiquated Alcatraz Island, its prison sitting atop a promontory that must have a great view, if not for the prisoners confined to cells years ago. Tourists often railed against this eyesore to an otherwise majestic bay setting. Maria found it emblematic of the psychologically imprisoned people she saw every day. At first, when she started her practice in San Francisco, she thought this general condition was due to the harried life of today's city population. However, Maria saw just as many patients from the more pastoral Marin County. But she soon realized, especially after voicing this concern with colleagues at symposiums here and abroad, that our computer-based society was definitely affecting or altering people's consciousness and affecting their feeling function. This allows one to establish proper values, and that lack is more evident in today's society than ever.

The lights on the wharf sparkled to life as the sun sank below the horizon to the west. Although she could not see its descent into the netherworld from this vantage point, she had always looked for the so-called "green flash" at sunset when sitting on her hillside home's west-facing patio. This phenomenon was caused by the sunlight streaming through the green-tinted ocean water. So far, it had eluded her, if not the denizens from that realm that popped up daily in her analysands' sessions.

Her reverie brought her back to Catherine Dumont and her "waking dreams." If these episodes were populated with a mother or father figure, most common among twentysomething analysands, she could address it from that angle. But that wasn't the case here. Instead, they sounded more like the universal imagery in dreams forecasting a disastrous event, like the assassination of a leader or a natural disaster, such as an earthquake or tsunami. So did the exploding grapefruit possibly presage an upheaval in this young woman's life, or maybe a collective one?

Maria's meal was served, and her glass of wine was refilled. She noticed the salad she had ignored and took a few bites. As always, the fish was prepared to perfection. Eating it helped to settle her. Was it some anxiety she was feeling? Maria asked herself. Sometimes the numinosity or spiritual affects of an evocative analysand's session bled into her "afterlife," as she liked to call her time off. And so, why was this dreamlike imagery so compelling to her? Despite Catherine's claim to the contrary, what balancing or compensatory insight did they offer this young woman? So she experienced episodes from other people's lives. Maybe it wasn't the content but the process that was important here. Did she have them to induce more sympathy for others? But if that were the case, wouldn't Dumont have been more cold and unemotional? While they were a curiosity for now, what if they continued and became persistent and threatened to overwhelm the conscious self? Yes, this would be more critical. Maria stopped eating and looked out at the bay's now-dark waters. Suddenly an Old Testament quote arose that Jung often used regarding Numinosum, Latin for numinosity, regarding his own deep unconscious upsurges, came to her: "It's a fearful thing to fall into the hands of the living God."

"Oh, my God," Maria exclaimed.

The waiter passing by her table stopped. "Is there something wrong with the fish, ma'am?"

Maria glanced up at his young face. "No, just a wayward thought."

He smiled. "That must've been some thought."

Maria could only say, "Yes, indeed."

2

It was already dark when Catherine arrived home in Mill Valley from her Friday afternoon session with Dr. Amidala. She parked her red Mustang around the back of the two-story hillside house and took the stairs to her second-floor apartment. Her landlord, Jeff Seymour, wasn't home yet, and given that it was Friday, she figured he was probably out with his girlfriend, Stephanie. So the house was quiet, and Cat, as she called herself, could take her time fixing dinner and just grab a beer and sit out on the back porch. Yes, after today's psychological session, she needed some alone time. She slipped out of her business casual straight black pants and white bishop-sleeve blouse and changed into yoga pants and a vintage *Jefferson Airplane* T-shirt. Cat set her laptop on the room's desk, took a Corona from the minifridge, pulled on a sweater, and stepped out onto the deck.

The half-moon had just risen over the west peak of Mount Tamalpais, if you could call it a mountain. She grew up in Fort Collins, Colorado, on the east side of the Rocky Mountains. Now, those were real mountains, she told herself. Cat looked down as the porch lights on the westside homes came on. This sparkling illumination drew her back to today's therapy session in the doctor's dimly lit office, which was more personal than the first and rather irritating. Yes, Amidala was sensitive in her probing and analysis of last night's haunting nighttime dream. But Cat resented therapy's basic premise: that something was wrong with you that needed "fixing," and why she had stayed away from it, or until now. A colleague recommended this psychiatrist when she shared one of her waking dreams.

Catherine had always thought of herself as well-adjusted, and while she had her share of teenage angst and went through a normal rebellious stage, she was never a problem child like some of her friends. The real problem in her family was her ex-hippie and current New Age fanatical parents. "Just grow up, will you?" was Cat's often-recited rejoinder to some of their antics and beliefs. But she did join them at yoga class before it became fashionable, and she did meditate but preferred active meditation instead of sitting cross-legged and staring at her third eye. Really. While at the top of her class in most subjects, sports dominated her teenage years: field hockey, soccer, and volleyball. Cat even won a National Collegian award for her midfield position and a tryout with the women's Olympic soccer team, which she never followed up on. By then, her artistic training was more important to her.

After graduating from the University of Colorado Boulder, Catherine attended one of the country's best graphic design schools: the California College of the Arts in Oakland. While she had been drawing and painting since childhood, she wanted to apply her talent in a practical or real-world way. Of course, her dreamy parents thought their daughter was the next van Gogh and encouraged her to pursue the fine arts. But she wanted to live and work in today's world, not their fantasy cop-out. Finally, her father, Barry, just gave up and told her mother, Joyce, "What do you expect? She's a Capricorn." After that, Cat listened to online goat bleats and would answer such nonsense with "baas." After graduation, when she took a job with a Bay Area creative advertising agency, her parents considered her a lost cause, even if she made twice her father's salary.

The twilight's blue haze variegated by the moisture in the Bay Area's air brought back last night's disturbing dream. She was at a carnival with all the crowd noises, hucksters caterwauling, and garish lights. Cat stepped into the House of Mirrors, which usually distorted one's image, elongated horizontally or vertically. Her image bled into other people's faces, but as she hurried on and ignored them, their expressions became more distorted and seemingly angry. She tried to find an exit, but this maze of mirrors was endless. Finally, she just sat down and covered her eyes with her hands, but the images permeated her inner world and became a screen of multiple photos—hundreds and then thousands. Catherine screamed and woke up, her T-shirt top soaked with sweat.

Dr. Amidala's probing brought up her lack of connection to others in her life, from her estranged family to friends she ignored and men whose date offers she repeatedly turned down. The picture of a socially isolated young woman became apparent to her. Maria pointed out that our inner and outer connections to life sometimes mirror each other, and the lack in one area pointed to the other. At that point, she just wanted to scream again.

Cat stood up, tossed her beer bottle into the trash, and headed downstairs for a quick dinner. She had picked up some fresh salmon from the market today, baked a slice in the oven, and stir-fried some vegetables. While she could've eaten her dinner at the kitchen table, Cat knew that Jeff and Stephanie would be strolling into the house anytime, and she didn't want to socialize. She took her plate with a bottle of water up to the side table in her room. It was dark now, and she turned on a lamp and ate dinner on her side table by the window, looking out into the night. Cat finished her meal and washed the dish and silverware in her kitchenette sink.

When she heard Jeff's car pull up out front, Cat's first impulse was to turn on the TV or the stereo to drown out the love-making noises that would soon follow. They were both very fit and athletic and went at it vigorously, which sometimes astonished her. It had been a while since she had had a boyfriend and made love to one of them, and she was now definitely feeling the lack, especially with this couple's constant reminder.

Instead, Catherine just lay down on the bed and let their squeals of delight run through her. She did get her hot and bothered, but Cat resisted the temptation to masturbate, which would've been too participatory. She wasn't a voyeur, just longing for a connection after last night's dream and today's analysis of it. They both came with piercing "aaahs." But then, Cat felt a similar release of tension in her body. *How strange,* she thought. *Talk about participatory, like I'm connected to them at another level.* Whoa. Cat had almost fallen asleep when there came a knock at her door. She opened it, and Stephanie stood there, sweat pouring off her naked body, only in a pair of white panties, her breasts gleaming, her nipples erect.

"Cat, since you didn't play music this time, we wondered if you'd like to join Jeff and me for another round."

Catherine was astonished by this offer and couldn't help but stare at the woman's luscious breasts. "I, uh . . . I mean, thanks for . . ."

Suddenly Stephanie reached behind her neck and pulled Catherine into her body, kissing her passionately, her wet tongue halfway down her throat, her breasts pushing up against her. And then, to her surprise, Catherine cupped the girl's breasts and kissed her back before pulling away.

"Maybe some other time. Really."

"Oh, soon then." Steph turned and walked down the stairs to the first floor. Cat had to avert her eyes from the swishing movements of the girl's buttocks in the silk panties before closing the door. Catherine went to the minifridge, grabbed another beer, went out to the back deck, and sat down. What just happened, she asked herself. Cat had never had a homoerotic dream or encounter of any kind, and while playing girls' sports, there were plenty of opportunities. No, it was this damn therapy stirring up things she wasn't ready to handle. Okay, so she had sexual hang-ups, big deal.

That night Catherine had another troubling dream. The following day she took out Amidala's business card, called the after-hours and weekend number, and left a message. "Dr. Amidala, this is Catherine Dumont. I'm sorry, but I have to stop my therapy. Maybe later, but I can't deal with this right now."

Moments later, the woman came on the line. "Is this about last night's mountain dream?"

"Oh, my God," she cried out.

"Yes, indeed." Before Catherine could say anything, her analyst added, "Monday, my office, four o'clock. Be there."

CATHERINE LISTENED to Dr. Amidala's explanation of shared dreams and that they were much more common than people realized. She had seen Christopher Nolan's *Inception*, if not pertinent here. "Okay, I understand that this most often happens with couples or people with close ties, but we've just met."

Maria sat back in her chair and twirled a strand of hair. "There are documented cases of therapists and patients sharing a dream in a long-term analysis, but yes, more often, it's with someone close to you." She paused. "As you know, Freud looked back to childhood repression to ascertain the meaning of a dream, while Jung looked forward to what it said about a person's future."

Cat snickered. "You mean we're going to hike Mount Everest together?"

"Literally, no. We were trekking up a mountain to reach its peak, or this therapy's goal of individuation for you and maybe for me—wholeness."

"And the Abominable Snowman?"

"A shadow figure who appeared when we were separated and looked like he would attack us until we held hands and connected. We would call this the anima stage, and then he turned into the archetypal Wise Old Man, the mana stage, to help us on our journey. A remarkably quick progression." Later Maria would look back on this dream and how it foretold their headlong trek into the collective unknown.

"So we must take this journey together?"

"That you continue with your analysis." Catherine nodded her head. "But it's important to note that neither of us leads the other in the dream. This may be a rare interactive analysis that includes me or an early stage of some collective impulse."

Catherine nodded her head. This prospect made her feel more at ease, and she sat back in her chair.

"This dream, besides its shared aspect, would fall under what Jung called *The Prospective Function*, or it's indicative of a path, as I said, toward greater psychological integration. In these cases, he said the dream tells us that the unconscious or the collective unconscious is more prophetic or foreseeing than the conscious self."

"In other words, trust my dream and my therapy with you?" she asked tentatively. Trust was a big issue with her.

"You could say that."

Catherine looked down. "And my homoerotic encounter with Stephanie that happened earlier that evening?"

"That's a different issue."

She looked up, a little uncertain. The dream's hand-holding on her mind.

Amidala smiled. "Don't worry. You're not my type."

They both had a good laugh. "There's always a little transference in these cases. Here, even countertransference with a shared dream or it speaks to my inability to be completely objective. That would be the first for me."

"I see."

"So, shall we explore this situation with Stephanie?" Maria asked, but Catherine looked away. "There's nothing to be embarrassed about it. Sexuality in all its forms is the bedrock of any therapy."

"It's just that—it's like telling your mother you masturbate."

Maria nodded her head. "So, did you ever have that conversation with her?"

Cat sniggered. "She would've probably taken out her array of dildos and showed me how to use them."

"That's progressive."

"Which is exactly what she would have said," Cat added.

"And if you told her that you had kissed and fondled a girlfriend?"

"She wouldn't blink. Mom was an old hippie. Free love and all that."

Maria nodded her head. "Okay, so let's start there." She was impressed by how quickly this young woman had integrated first her shadow and then her animus in the dream. Then she realized that applied to her as well. Most interesting.

An hour later, Catherine walked out of Maria's inner office and had the receptionist set another appointment for the end of the week. After spewing out some of her sexual hang-ups and history, she felt a little shaky and decided to take a walk before driving home. Lafayette Park was three blocks away. She sat on a bench, looked over the green lawns, and meditated to clear her mind and her "energy field," as her father would say. Then, suddenly, Cat had another waking dream: *A young man wearing a British-cut suit was sitting at a desk working on a computer. It appeared he was arranging somebody's schedule. He looked up and peered in her direction. Then, he stopped as if he heard something distressing. He stood up, stepped over to a large oak door, and knocked on it. "Sir, is everything all right?"*

"Go back to your desk, you little pissant," someone barked from inside.

The man stood there and listened. He then heard the distinct click of a revolver's hammer. He opened the door, and an older gentleman, very distinguished-looking, had a gun to his head. The young man dove across the desk and tried to wrestle the gun out of his hand. It went off with a loud boom, shooting the young man in the shoulder. What appeared to be a musclebound security guy then rushed in, grabbed the gun, and laid the wounded man on the floor. He ripped off his shirt and used it to stanch the blood flow. The older man was in shock, and then the waking dream ended.

Catherine sat there for a long moment. She felt a great relief that this official had been saved and the young man wasn't killed. But what did this have to do with her? Why was she seeing the suicide attempt of a foreign dignitary? Then she had a thought. Did her presence somehow trigger the boy's quick response? She jumped up and walked back to Dr. Amidala's building in a daze. She stepped inside the office just as Maria came out, apparently leaving for the day.

Maria looked at her shaken analysand. "You had another one!"

"Yes. Someone important tried to kill himself." Catherine stood her ground. "What the hell is this about? I feel like I'm going crazy."

"No, you're not. You're waking up, and that can be a rough ride." Maria stepped over, took Catherine's arm, and walked her back into her office.

What was she trying to kill? Maria had to wonder.

3

Arlington, Virginia

Dr. Greg Mires strolled into the DARPA offices on Randolph Street, swiped his access card, and walked to the elevators. He looked like the other nerds here, short and bushy-haired with wire-rimmed glasses. When he first signed on with General Stanley Morton's SPS program, he was often mocked in the lobby and hallways by the sobriquet "Black Swan" by the "real" DARPA employees, as they liked to call themselves. "Or, is that BS for Bullshit?" someone once asked. The kidding stopped when he started taking pictures of them with his cell phone. He knew how to deal with bullies as a much-maligned brainiac during his primary school years. Most of these guys were hard-science geeks working on cutting-edge innovations with military applications. It was what they liked to call tomorrow's science or "science fiction," as his SPS colleagues said about their many out-on-the-limb failures.

His group was looking for what Nassim Nicholas Taleb classified as *Black Swan* events or trends in his book by that name published a while back. As General Stanley Morton liked to quote: "Almost everything important in social life is often produced by rare but consequential shocks and jumps; all the while, almost everything studied about social life focuses on the normal using the bell curve method." Morton sold the DOD on his program by citing scientific discoveries like the Global Internet, personal computers, cell phones, and events like 9/11 and the Bolshevik takeover of Russia in 1918 that fit this category. It was now Mire's and his team of researchers' task to find the needle in this proverbial haystack of unexpected but possibly high-impact developments.

While Morton sold the DOD on his program, it was selling DARPA's Director Charlotte Blackman on housing it there that was the challenge, or so the general told Greg during his recruitment. Morton had worked with her in Army Intelligence back in the late 1980s. She had read Taleb's book and was familiar with the Bayesian Probability theory that the unexpected development of some phenomena can't be predicted by frequency or propensity analysis. So Blackman asked the gray-haired General in his medals-studded uniform for an example.

"What if young children here or abroad working on computers start to develop extremely high IQs?"

"Sounds win-win to me."

"Yes, but what if these supersmart kids begin to dominate the population base everywhere until they start to look at the rest of us as useless and/or threatening."

"Ah. I see. The AI proposition in computer science applied socially."

She looked at his prospective list of employees. "And your people are mostly feeling-intuitive types?" The General nodded his head. He had been at the forefront of using the Myers-Briggs personality typing in the military years ago.

Morton could see the wheels churning. "I have my own funding."

"You won't fall under the purview of any of our technical offices; you'll just be housed here?" Morton nodded his head. "So, Stanley, you want your people to rub shoulders with our science geeks to keep them focused on the big picture?"

"Yes, and you might find they'll rub off on them."

Blackman shook her head. "God Forbid."

Getting off the elevator, Mires walked to their four-office suite at the end of the hallway. As always, he stopped and stared at the stenciled letters on the door: SPS, which stood for Sociological, Psychological, Spiritual. Early on, one of their disclaimers had snuck up after hours and taped a banner over it: Stupid Plus Stupid. Unfortunately for him, the hallway camera had caught this prank, and the young man was suspended for two weeks. *Stupid begets stupid reactions*, Greg had thought at the time. He now stepped inside and saw that his crew was already fast at work. He was the multi-disciplinarian of the group: a Ph.D. in psychology with a minor in social psychology and a Zen Buddhist with a master's in religion. He went to the kitchen, poured a cup of green tea, and then headed to his office.

One of his mavens was a social media expert who came in early every day to post a rundown of possible relevant SM and other postings. Emily Norton, a spy novel aficionado, had suggested that her report mirror the PDB (President's Daily Brief) on overnight security issues. Eric Darby, formerly an analyst for the National Security Council, who had overseen one of their twenty-year Global Trends reports, had gotten her a presidential coffee cup from the White House. It was his way of asserting himself since his statistical data reporting was the opposite of their intuitive methodology. "Darby's here to keep you honest," Morton had told them.

Emily had friended, or when denied access, hacked the Facebook accounts of thousands of movers and shakers and the organizational websites in all fields of interest. But, of course, scanning through the "social muck" of these accounts every day could warp any advanced thinker. So Darby, a math geek, created an algorithmic with variable and adjustable parameters to do her raw web search. When he showed her how to operate it, the pert bespectacled young woman, her black glasses sliding down her nose as she leaned over her desk, showing some cleavage, told the thirtysomething, "I could kiss you."

To which the tall, lanky, often acerbic statistician stepped closer and replied, "Well, what's stopping you?" Emily blushed and turned back to her computer screen and its first data download.

Today, Greg went through Emily's daily briefing, which was like a collective unconscious outcry about environmental pollution, rampant racism, downward economic trends, socialist programs, and other concerns along this line. Then, he spotted something of interest. He called Alicia Holmes, their cross-disciplined psychological savant.

"Alicia, have you read Emily's GDB yet (Greg's Daily Briefing)?"

"Yeah, I saw the child's daydream item too."

At first Greg had figured that as someone so attuned to the psychological substrata of people and events, Alicia was naturally psychic. This ability was later confirmed time and again.

"A child having a daydream of an actual event in another child's life. What would cause that?"

"If it were in the same social subset, like a classroom or even a school, I'd say it was psychic contamination, like spreading around a cold virus, but this school psychologist reported that it was about a little boy in a nearby city. Which she followed up on and confirmed."

Greg could almost see her nod her head. "This sounds interesting. Let's check out this . . ."

"Anomalous Event," Alicia added.

"I'll get everybody looking into it. Tell Emily to do another more specific search on telepathic incidents here and abroad. See if this is happening elsewhere. And Alicia . . ."

"Pack a bag."

Greg joked, "And be sure to wash your hands after the interview."

After nine months, this was their first real lead of any kind. Greg knew not to alert the general. Like most in the military, the man wasn't interested in speculation but in results, and it didn't matter to Morton how off-kilter they were. He next typed an email blast to everybody in the office about this search focus. Greg sat back in his chair. After a moment, he closed his eyes and could almost feel the energy strata around him shift.

As a boy he could always sense this kind of movement in what he would now call the "ethers," even if that term was a bit antiquated. He had figured that people and events were driven by more than mental or psychological factors, as his teachers would emphasize. He couldn't quite figure that out, but he knew that little Jimmy Cantor wasn't getting a bike for Christmas, given his deplorable behavior. When he told the boy as much and it was proven true, Jimmy called him "witch boy," which seemed to catch on with the kids. He could remember walking with his mother as they passed a student on their way home from church. The boy called out, "I didn't know witches went to church." His mother questioned that, and he told her about a movie he had seen and talked up at school. It wasn't until the eighth grade that his world expanded when a book on Eastern philosophy fell off the shelf at the public library in front of him. The term "karma" helped to explain some of his intuitions.

Dayton, Ohio

The principal of this north Dayton elementary school, James Jacobs, mid-fifties, his balding spot combed over, a striped shirt at odds with his plaid pants, studied the parent's permission slip. He then glanced over at Alicia Holmes and shook his head. "I'm puzzled, Ms. Holmes. Our school psychologist reports an incident to her governing association, NASP, and a week later, a government researcher shows up to question the child."

"As you can see, we first queried his father, Major Mark Bernard, at Wright Patterson, for his permission."

Jacobs looked over at a stout and prim Margret Bayer in her long green ankle-length dress, who seemed as mystified. "James, I'm required to report . . . unusual behavior or incidents. Never thought they would post it, and it would come to this."

The principal turned back to Holmes. "Come to what, I'd like to know?" he asked peevishly.

"A child daydreaming about an actual incident in another child's life at a distant city drew our curiosity."

"Who exactly do you work for again, Ms. Holmes?"

"As I said, The Department of Education."

Jacobs looked down at her business card. "And they're interested in children's daydreams? There must be something else going on here?"

Alicia gave this bureaucrat her best steely stare. "If you prefer, I could interview the child at his home, but I'd like your psychologist to sit in on it here."

Jacobs glanced at Bayer. "I think that's the better proposition, James."

The principal nodded his head. "Okay. Margret set up the interview for this afternoon and take Ms. Holmes to lunch in the cafeteria." He smiled. "It's Tuesday, macaroni and cheese."

"Yummy."

After she had finished half her meal and pushed it aside, Alicia turned to Bayer. "Tell me a little about David Bernard."

"After the incident, I talked with his homeroom teacher, and she reported that he's an excellent student but something of a daydreamer."

"Maybe he's smarter than she thinks and is bored."

Margaret nodded. "I thought as much and checked his last IQ test, over 130, though that's hard to gauge at this age."

"He's eleven years old?"

"Yes, and socially something of a misfit, which is unusual given his background. I mean, you would think he'd fall in line with his military family."

"So you're on the genetic side of the nature versus nurture argument," Alicia probed.

"In his case, I think both would apply."

"You know, there could be a third influence impacting this child."

Margret looked mystified again. "Really? Whatever could that be?"

"That's what I'm here to investigate."

An hour later, Alicia looked across the table at David Bernard, rather delicate-looking with dreamy eyes. His brown hair was cut short but not as severe as his father's military buzz cut from his online Air Force photo.

"Am I in trouble?" he asked after Margret introduced Ms. Holmes as a fellow psychologist. "Did I do something wrong?"

"No, David. Not at all. We're just curious about your daydream of the little boy falling off his slide," Alicia said.

"Like I told Mrs. Bayer, it just came to me out of the blue."

"You were sitting on the sidelines watching a field hockey match?" she asked.

"Yes. I don't like sports, but the gym teacher makes me suit up."

"Do you resent that?" He looked back at her. "Does it make you mad?"

"No. I like to watch, as long as I don't have to play. I mean, half the time, the boys come away with scraped knees and bruises."

Alicia nodded her head and looked down at the incident report. "Like the little boy who fell off the slide."

"I felt bad for him. His knee was bleeding."

"Before you had this daydream, had any of the boys in the match that day scraped their knee?"

David thought for a moment. "Yes. I remember that." He paused. "Is that why I saw the other boy?"

"We really don't know. But, let me ask, is this the first daydream like that you've had?"

"Yes. I daydream about places I've been to or people I've met, but nothing like this before." He paused for a long moment. "But someone once daydreamed about me."

Both women leaned forward. "Was that someone in school here?" Alicia asked. This exploration was getting more interesting.

David shrugged his shoulders. "Nobody I know. One day, I was walking home from school, about to cross a street, when a car zoomed around the corner. I didn't see it coming, but I . . . saw an image of a blond-headed girl shaking her head. I stopped just in time." He paused. "I guess I was relieved, as mom always says, but I did feel different afterward. Better. Like someone was watching over me. A Guardian Angel."

This occurrence brought David's dream experience to another level. A child drawn across time and space by another child's injury was one thing. But a forewarning of a life-threatening accident was something altogether different. Somebody somewhere, and a little girl at that, could sense or foretell a disastrous event and intercede.

Alicia asked, "David, did you see this girl clearly?"

He nodded his head again. Alicia turned to Bayer. "I'd like to bring in a sketch artist to get a drawing of her."

"Definitely. You've piqued my interest now."

Yes, Alicia thought as Bayer walked little David Bernard back to his classroom. She sat in the counselor's office and considered her initial impression of the boy. He was definitely in tune with the "broader reality," as she had called it since childhood. This excursion was the first time she had returned to an elementary school, and just walking the halls here and seeing the mix of children brought back her psychic experiences as a young girl. Alicia could "sense" things that at first alarmed her. She was the top student in her high school and got a National Merit Scholarship in her senior year. But these impressions didn't compute, as her math teacher would say, which led to years of doubt on her part. It wasn't until she entered Duke University and studied their parapsychology data from 1930 to 1965 that she could fit it into a new paradigm. She sensed that David Bernard wouldn't have to wait that long.

Bayer stepped back into her office. Alicia stood up and gathered her laptop and purse. "Let me walk you out to your car."

On the way out, she told Alicia that Jacobs would call the local police station to see if they could get a sketch artist to draw a picture of David's "mysterious" visitor. Alicia chuckled at that description as if it were an ET encounter. They said their goodbyes with promises to keep in touch.

The police artist came the next day and rendered a lifelike drawing of the little girl she emailed to Holmes. But what really interested Jacobs and Bayer was when a security officer from Wright Patterson showed up and made them sign national security non-disclosure agreements. Afterward, the principal turned to Bayer, "I told you there was something else going on here."

Bayer nodded her head. "Yeah. Holmes is no school psychologist."

4

London, England

Evelyn Richardson, her loose hanging skin marred with brown spots, looked out the thin pane of the cross-shaped window at her University of London, Birkbeck College office. It was located in one of its older stone buildings dating back to the 1800s. It was the beginning of the fall 2021 semester, and she watched the students scurrying by on the walkways and shook her head. This Jungian analyst and teacher of Analytical Psychology had taught here for some forty years, well before the college's modern facelift with its newer steel and glass buildings. Carl Jung and his Bollinger Tower with its gleaming white stone, where she had first met him while in training, came to mind as a comparison. Jung would shake his head, taking a pull on his antique Swiss pipe, if he saw her teaching in one of these 200-seat auditoriums. But then, much of modern life had seemingly passed her by, and she would tell colleagues and students good riddance to it. The Soul needs earth and stone to be awakened in these students.

She now picked up the *Jung Journal* from San Francisco and reread the inquiry by Dr. Maria Amidala about "waking dreams," asking if other therapists were encountering analysand's episodes of this nature. Evelyn set down the journal and slapped her leg. She remembered Maria well, a real Italian spitfire. It would be just like her to attract something of this nature. Of course, Jung first used the term years ago to describe his encounters with the personal and collective unconscious, but Evelyn sensed that her former student had unearthed a new expression of it. She looked over at her antique, mahogany longcase grandfather clock and checked the time; it would be too early to phone Maria in California, so she'd wait until she got home and ate dinner.

Evelyn had to wonder if her analysand, Fyodor Makarov, the Russian dissident, referred to her by another psychiatrist treating his schizophrenia with clozapine, wasn't as delusional as Hardgrave had insisted. The man's hallucinations often centered around Vladimir Putin, the Russian president. As a KGB agent in the 1980s, he had targeted Fyodor's father, who was eventually imprisoned as a mental patient for his protests against the communist system. Makarov and his mother fled to England, where his father had stashed a small fortune from his illegal dealings in Russia and East Germany. Fyodor graduated from Oxford with a degree in political science. He became a journalist and an author who first supported Boris Yeltsin and his new democratic Russia and its shift to a market economy. However, this allowed the rise of the wealthy oligarchs who gobbled up much of the country's prized properties and industries and led to Putin's rise to power as prime minister in 1999. Makarov's theory was that a group of KGB agents had seen the fall of the Soviet Union coming and had pilfered state monies meant for the satellite countries of the Eastern Block and used it to take over some Russian industries.

Makarov claimed to have survived two assassination attempts by poisoning in 2005 and 2013, which the Russian press called book promotions. However, given his father's schizophrenia and possibly his mother's, he was forced into psychiatric treatment by his wife and adult children. Apparently, the drug helped stem his sometimes aberrant behavior, but his doctor couldn't deal with the man's hallucinations. Hardgrave knew how Carl Jung had worked with his psychosis, or hearing voices and seeing visions, in his late thirties, which led to his discovery and use of the archetypes of the Collective Unconscious. He told Richardson such therapy might help his patient. Evelyn was treating him, and they made some progress until Makarov had a vision not strictly derived from his unconscious mind and was, he claimed, an actual event. He saw Putin in his Kremlin office talking about his constitutional revisions of 2020, which seemed to point to his stepping down in 2024. He told his cronies not to worry—that he would create a crisis that required him to stay in office. But this wasn't dream imagery in the usual sense.

Evelyn hit the button on her phone's intercom. "Millie. Call Fyodor Makarov tomorrow and schedule a session with him for the end of the week. Find a suitable opening in my class schedule."

"Yes, ma'am."

She grabbed her purse and book bag with its essays to grade at home and sighed. "I'm getting too old for this donkey work. I need a grad student like Maria to help with it, but they're all so dense now. Christ."

Her third-floor flat on Charlotte was only a few blocks away. As she hurried through the courtyard to the street, several students waved, but Evelyn didn't recognize any of them. Maybe she needed new glasses or more captivating students. There was a light drizzle, and Evelyn pulled her green Manchester raincoat closer to her body. She would complain, but when did it not rain in London. In a foul mood, she asked herself the cause. Feeling her way to the core of her upset, Evelyn could sense it was the proposed session with

Makarov. *Talk about dense and dreary*, she thought. He was like one of those Russian nesting dolls, but she could never get beyond the first layer with him. Now his so-called waking dream might draw her deeper inside. "Thanks, Maria," she complained out loud.

When Evelyn called, Dr. Amidala was in a session but said she would call back in half an hour. She did so promptly on the hour. They exchanged greetings and pleasant catch-ups, and then her former student asked in her usual direct manner:

"Okay, Evelyn. I guess you read my inquiry in the *Jung Journal* and have some follow-up?"

The old dame laughed. "I could always count on you to get to the point. But you're not concerned that I'm calling about a health issue?"

"Which you would never share with anybody."

"You know me well. Memorial service notices only. No, I have a schizoid analysand who claimed to have had one of these 'waking dreams.'"

"And you've dismissed it so far as him being delusional?"

"Yes, my dear. But then what the man saw had a real-world confirmation in the . . . political arena. I won't say more than that."

"Interesting. My analysand saw something in that arena too."

"Russia?" Evelyn asked tentatively.

"No, in England and pretty dramatic."

Evelyn caught her breath. "Oh, my God. I think I know what they saw. They kept it quiet, but you hear things." She paused to collect herself. "Let's not say anymore over the phone. Are you coming to the Fall Jung Symposium?"

"I wasn't until now."

"It's filling up, so book it soon and plan to stay with me."

"I hate to put you out, Evelyn."

"No doubt the hotel rooms are all bugged, I would imagine. And I still have a spare bedroom."

"Okay. I'll see you in November." Maria paused. "There's something else. Maybe a countertransference issue with my 'waking dream' analysand. We're having shared nighttime dreams."

"That's interesting. Anything else?"

"No. It's strictly professional."

Richardson sighed. "My dear, while this isn't the freewheeling 1980s where psychologist/patient boundaries got crossed regularly, go where the unconscious leads you, especially with something this unorthodox."

They said their goodbyes, and Evelyn hung up her landline. She didn't have a cell phone because it gave people too much access, especially the snoops at MI5. They had roped her into analyzing Soviet defectors during the late Cold War era in cooperation with MI6. She made the mistake of working with them on a couple of cases and even established a psychological profile that proved useful, as her handler confided. But she didn't like their deceitful tactics and refused to cooperate after one harrowing case.

FYODOR MAKAROV SULLENLY SAT across from Richardson in his upholstered chair with a table between them for drinks. She had been grilling him about his waking dream of the Russian president: the time, the office arrangement, the weather outside, a description of the people there, and what they were wearing.

"So, Madame Richardson, I take it that you believe me now?"

"I've gotten confirmation of something like this happening to others."

Makarov was a big bear of a man with a close-cut black beard and hair, both graying. And he always wore a tailored suit, this one blue. He seemed to have a perpetual cold and blew his nose during sessions. Quite annoying. He now leaned forward and stared at her, then nodded his head. "Someone else is having these kinds of daydreams?"

"Yes, apparently."

The man shook his head in disgust. "It took that kind of confirmation to convince you. So I'll have to cut my hand off to prove that I'm bleeding somewhere else?"

Evelyn didn't take the bait. She leaned forward, her birdlike finger tapping the armrest. "Tell me, Fyodor. Did you take your meds the day you had this vision?"

He glared at her, disgusted. "You say you believe me, but now you're asking if it's a schizoid delusion. Make up your fucking mind, lady."

"No, that's not the case. I'm wondering if the medication suppresses them."

He looked back hopefully and questioned her, "You'd take me off the meds?"

She shook her head. "I'm just a consulting doctor, in this case, brought in to deal with what Dr. Hardgrave considers your 'delusions.'"

"You know I put in a good word about you to Dr. Hardass. Some of the older Russian dissidents remember you from the 80s."

Evelyn quickly changed the subject; she didn't want to drag up that history. "Tell me, have you had other episodes like this?" The man paused, then shook his head but looked down. "Fyodor, you must be honest with me if you want to shed light on why this is coming up."

He furiously spat out, "That one came up because of what Putin did to my father, family, and homeland."

"Fyodor, the other episodes."

Makarov took a deep breath. "Just one, a while back. It's embarrassing—about an old girlfriend from my 20s. Saw her taking a shower and slipping on a bar of soap, then catching herself. She's fat and ungainly now, but Lana smiled at me as if I were there. I guess it brought back memories of happier times because I felt delighted."

"So you have a personal connection to both of these . . . subjects."

He nodded his head; he knew what that meant: dream analysis. "Now you're telling me they're like any other dream?"

"Not exactly, but like in all dreamwork, we look for common denominators."

Fyodor nodded his head. "I didn't take my meds that day either."

Then it dawned on her. "Did you tell anybody in the dissident community about this Kremlin episode?"

"Yes. I wondered if anybody else was having them since we are all harassed by the Russian SVR."

Evelyn sat back in her chair. "I don't want to alarm you, but for your safety, can you go back and tell them that it was just a delusional dream?"

Makarov thought about her concern and sighed. "Of course, the old Russian psychic experiments, remote viewing, and all that crap." He paused. "Oh, shit. If they think I can remote-view Putin's inner office conversations . . ." He abruptly stood up. "Thank you, doctor. This session has been most helpful, but I have arrangements to make."

With that, the man turned and stormed out of her inner office. Evelyn sat back and thought through this situation for a long moment. While her analysand had broken the confidentiality of their sessions by sharing his waking dream with compatriots, she felt complicit by first treating it as a delusion. What if his claims of assignation attempts were also factual? Given that the SVR was monitoring Russian dissidents here, what if this prediction got back to the Kremlin? Either way, she had to protect Makarov.

Evelyn took a key from her keychain, opened the bottom right-side drawer of her desk, and removed a lockbox. She then took out an old battered red address book, found the number, and placed a call. She figured MI5 would still be monitoring these old numbers. It rang a couple of times, and there were several clicks. Finally, a young woman's voice came on the line.

"Can I help you?"

"I know it's been decades, but this is the number of my old handler Jason Lewis." There was a long silence, and she could hear the woman typing in the name.

"I'm sorry, ma'am, but Mr. Lewis was retired and died two years ago. Can someone else help you?"

"My name is Dr. Evelyn Richardson. I used to analyze Russian dissidents for you back in the late 80s. Something has come up."

"Please hold."

Almost five minutes passed when an older man's crusty voice came on the phone. "Richardson. I thought you'd be dead by now. Can't say that would be any sweat off my balls after what you pulled."

"Who's this, Harris? How charming." The man didn't respond. "Look. Something's come up, information from an analysand, a Russian dissident, who may have what you could say is an inside pipeline to Putin."

Harris huffed. "What? He dreams about him. Who doesn't? At least half the guys on the Russian desk at MI6 do."

"It's not that, and I'm only calling because he may be in danger. He saw something, what appeared to be an actual meeting in the Kremlin. Check it out, but I'm not working with you shitbirds again."

"Likewise." There was a long pause. "I'll have one of our young shitbirds drop by tomorrow. You at the same university address?"

"Tell him to call this number and make an appointment. I have teaching and patient schedules."

"You better not be pulling my chain, Richardson. I can still make things difficult for you."

Evelyn hung up the phone, wondering if she had made the right call. She had bad memories of her work with them in the late 1980s, especially one case where she had inadvertently trapped a Russian dissident into confessing that he was a double agent. While they gave her accolades for a job well done, the man was sent to prison for twenty years; his family returned to Russia and was mistreated there, as Harris had told her. It felt like she had violated the spirit of the Hippocratic Oath to uphold ethical standards in regard to patients, despite extenuating circumstances. She refused to work with MI5/6 after that. They hounded her for a couple of years, but after the fall of the Soviet Union, they let up. Evelyn visited Yuri Yegorov in prison every year until he hung himself. The prison psychologist told her the location of his unmarked grave, where she still placed flowers in the spring and prayed for his forgiveness.

5

Novosibirsk, Russia

At first, primary school teacher Arina Dorzhiev dismissed little Elena Mongush's concern about her driving home that day. She assured the ten-year-old that she had lived in the Novosibirsk Oblast in Siberia all her life, her family for generations, and she could navigate the early-winter weather just fine. And then, a car back-ended her VW Polo at an intersection, pushing it into the path of a truck, which she barely avoided by quickly downshifting, hitting the gas pedal, and driving out of the crossroad. Arina pulled her car to the curb and felt like getting out and cursing at this asshole, as she was prone to do. But she just shook her head, her red curls twisting beneath her orange wool cap. She could almost sense Elena's presence. *Let it go*, she told herself. *It's not worth it.* The other driver drove past, looked mortified, and mouthed, *izvinite pojaluista* (I'm sorry). That was good enough for her. She drove away feeling "protected."

That night she told her father Ivan about her near accident and Elena's warning. While getting older, his mind was still as sharp as she remembered as a child. He worked as a software engineer, a second career. He reminded her that Akademgorodok, the city's "Academic Town" and scientific center, was the site of Russian parapsychology experiments going back to the 1960s and 70s.

"What does that have to do with anything."

"After the fall of the Soviet Union, most of those scientists stayed here and found other work, some even in my company. I knew about their psychotronic magnetic wave experiments, like the antenna they discovered in Boris Yeltsin's office, somebody's attempt—maybe the old KGB in the FSB—to affect his mind. There was speculation that psychotronic devices could also cause genetic mutations in the germline and get passed on to their subject and experimenter's offspring."

Arina just shook her head. "Dad, you've been watching too many American sci-fi movies. We're not part of the *Matrix*."

"Okay, *umnye brucki* (smarty-pants), but look into her family."

Yes, she thought, *but don't look too deeply into ours.* Arina had always had a problematic relationship with her father, one of those "state scientists." Growing up, she could sense that he was driven by his past work for the Russian military during the communist era and fearful that his expertise would one day be called upon again. Of course, he wouldn't talk about it with anybody, and it seemed to hold back his expression of love for Arina and her mother, Karina. She had died two years ago from a lonely heart, she felt, despite her cancer. After that, her father opened up a bit more, and their relationship improved, especially living under the same roof. Grief will do that to you. But Ivan still jumped every time somebody knocked on the front door.

The next day Arina checked the girl's file and discovered that her grandfather had indeed been a military scientist. She logged onto Yandex, the web browser, and read about Dr. Yuri Mongush and the military unit 71592. There was a chilling quote from a recent academic paper ". . . according to calculations made in 1974, the generator Radioson can effectively treat a city of a hundred square kilometers, plunging its inhabitants into a deep sleep."

That afternoon Arina met with the petite and strangely ethereal girl and asked about her premonition of this incident.

"I sometimes see things, like in a dream, but while awake."

"So you saw my car get hit by a truck?"

"I just saw a car hit the rear end of your car." So it was psychic precognition, but she felt the girl's presence there.

Arina nodded her head. "So that wasn't the first time you saw something like that?"

Elena shook her head, her long blond hair swaying back and forth. "No, I see things all the time. It started months ago." Her teacher gave the girl a questioning look. "Just ask the other kids. Some have them too."

She reported her conversation to the principal Dima Kozlov, a psychologist forced into school administration because of a failed private practice in recent years. The harried, narrow-faced man shook his head. "Arina, I thought you were more levelheaded. So the little girl says she saw your car getting rear-ended. You know how many car accidents happen every day here in the winter?"

"A few, I guess."

"If the girl says a meteorite will hit our town tomorrow, and it does, I'll look into it. But, for now, I have to figure out how to feed these little urchins with the new budget cuts."

Arina looked over at him, and she could sense the fear driving him. She had heard that his practice had dried up because of "inappropriate" behavior with his patients. The teacher who told her added, "It wasn't sexual, so you don't have to worry about that." He just got too friendly with the women. Another lonely heart. Maybe Dima should have met her mother.

Arina nodded and didn't say that neither of them might survive such a disaster. Her father would be proud of her smarty-pants restraint. So she dropped her inquiry and never followed up by asking the other students if they "saw things." With the winter weather's encroachment, gym classes were moved to the basketball court, including volleyball. Then one day, weeks later, Arina heard an ambulance pull up to the school, and a boy hit in the face with the volleyball was rushed to the hospital. Arina was watching the ambulance pull away at her classroom window when Elena stepped over.

"I told Dimitri not to play today, but he wouldn't listen. He likes to spike the ball at people."

"You saw him get hit in the face with a volleyball?"

The little girl nodded her head. "He's going to have a lump in his nose. Too bad. He was such a pretty boy. Maybe he'll like me now."

The following day she asked her third-level class if anybody ever saw things like in a dream, but when wide awake, that actually happened. All the kids glanced at each other, wondering about this inquiry. "I ask because Elena told Dimitri not to play volleyball yesterday, and we know what happened." She could feel a hesitancy with the children. "I mean, it's a good thing, and nobody will get in trouble for it. I'm just curious." Finally, Gregor and Katya raised their hands.

After school that day, she talked with both of them and wrote down their daydreams about incidents that happened simultaneously or came about later. There were two for Gregor and one for Katya. The boy added, "We're not spying on them, and it makes all of us feel better."

"How's that?" Arina asked.

"It's like we get to know them from the inside out."

Arina looked at Elena. "Is that what you experience too?"

"Yes. I just love everybody afterward." How interesting. They're merging.

Then, that night after dinner, she reported her findings to her father.

"So you have three kids in one homeroom of thirty reporting these daydream events happening in other children's lives?"

"The first girl, Elena, says hers started last summer, and she has one every couple months or so, and the other two have had three altogether."

"Statistically, that rates as highly significant." He paused and gave this some thought. "And your principal, this Dima Kozlov, just dismissed the girl's visions as coincidental?" Arina nodded her head. "I don't think you should take it any further. I mean, this Kozlov could fire you. I'll ask around at work with some of the old guard. Russian intelligence might be interested in psychic children if that's what this is."

"I don't want to get these children rounded up, as they used to do, or what we read about the old days," Arina said in alarm.

"Don't' worry. I'll make it general like, 'I hear that kids around here have daydreams of others that come true. You ever hear anything like that?' That should get run up the line, or not, but it keeps everybody's name out of it."

Arina nodded her head. "Thanks, Dad. That sounds better." But she still felt a pang of regret having told him about it. Such a disclosure sounded like the old reporting syndrome from the communist era she had read about.

Moscow, Russia

Yuri Belov, his dark hair cut short, medium height with an athletic built, was the head of the Russian FSB's (Internal Security) Science and Technical Service Department at its headquarters in Lubyanka Square. He reread the resident agent's report from their regional office in Novosibirsk, Siberia. He shook his head. As an Honors graduate from the *Moscow Institute of Physics and Technology,* he considered these field agents as educated and informed as the old KGB thugs. He had to laugh. "There are rumors of children having daydreams of events that happen." He felt like asking if he could get some stock tips from them.

"What's so funny," Galina Ilyin, his emergent science officer, asked. In her thirties but trim and fit from weekly gym visits, she looked at Yuri. Her desk was close to his in this open-office arrangement. They didn't have much space, with Counterespionage and Border Services increasingly getting the priority.

"Some airhead in Novosibirsk reports children having daydreams of actual events. Probably boys having wet dreams about the girl's bathrooms."

Galina smirked and added, "Yuri, was that what you dreamed about in primary school?"

"Didn't have to. The science guys rigged up remote pinhole cameras in the girls' showers."

"That's really disgusting," she scoffed. Then she gave this report some thought. "You know that's where they conducted the country's psychic research back when. Remote hypnosis, telepathy, precognition."

"Oh yeah, that would've been considered emerging science in its day."

"We did study it in school. And it wasn't as absurd as some now think."

"Okay, I'll send the log over to you. But don't waste too much time on it. And Galina, let me know if you start daydreaming about me."

"You wish," she said. Galina said no more. She had to keep a wrap on sexual banter with all the hard male cases in the building. This concern was why she cut her brown hair short and kept her uniform dress long. The file appeared in her email folder, and Galina opened and read the report. She shook her head. One line in a rumor list of local scuttlebutt, as the GRU guys would characterize it. Like Yuri, most science officers would readily dismiss such rumors. But she had always been fascinated with parapsychology and attempts to apply it to security work. This lead was probably a dead end; maybe she was just bored with their routine scientific research: BBBs: bigger and better bombs, she called it. Why not take a chance and follow up on it.

Galina highlighted the agent's name, Kostya Stepanov, and the number for the FSB regional office. They were four hours ahead of them, 3:00 in the afternoon there. She used the office's secure long-distance phone line. Galina identified herself, and the call was routed to this officer. He was surprised that this odd item would attract anybody's interest at headquarters.

"Agent Stepanov, who passed this rumor along to you?"

"One of the old guard at Sibers, the software company, probably a former state scientist, told me somebody was passing around this rumor."

"Did he say who?"

"No, and I didn't ask. You hear this kind of crap all the time. I just thought it would lighten the mood back there; I mean, with everything else happening." He paused. "Who exactly are you, Officer Ilyin?"

"I work in the Scientific and Technical Service Department."

"Really, and you think this might be credible, or is somebody poking fun at me or punking me, as the Americans say?"

"Trust me. I'm taking it very seriously, and I want you to get the name of this rumormonger and bring him in for questioning tomorrow."

"You're kidding."

Galina deepened her voice. "Do I sound like I'm kidding, Stepanov?"

"No, you sound like a real ballbuster. I'll follow up on it."

Galina hung up the phone. Yuri looked over at her. "Damn. You really are taking this to heart. Just get results you can report."

"Yuri, have you ever read the book *The Black Swan?*"

"I thought all swans were white?"

Galina shook her head in dismay, and she worked for this guy. She briefly explained the theory and how it has been used to explain unforeseen events and trends.

Yuri just shook his head. "Sounds like a reach to me, but that's your field, so dig your own grave." Galina winched at this slight.

She now called up the FSB online library on her computer, Western magazine subcategory, and typed in the keywords "daydreams," "visions," and "hallucinations." It was tapped into an uncensored version of Google for Western inquiries. Galina got back several current references and looked through them, following up on the most promising. Then, she came upon a request in the San Francisco *Jung Journal*, asking if any psychiatrists had encountered analysand's "waking dreams." She made another library search in Western psychological literature on this topic. It returned references to Carl Jung's work, which she was familiar with from university courses on psychology.

She read excerpts exploring this subject in his books and papers about his work with Active Imagination. So she figured Dr. Amidala had a patient experiencing this phenomenon, whatever it was. She next did an FSB web biographical search on this Amidala. Galina read through her background and came up with a former teacher, Dr. Evelyn Richardson, in London. This name created a redline alert. Richardson was a former MI5 asset who had analyzed Soviet dissidents in the 1980s and was currently in analysis with the Russian dissident and high-valued target Fyodor Makarov. This track was getting interesting. These were credible scientists.

The next day the always gruff Stepanov came back to her with the name of the rumormonger, Ivan Dorzhiev, a software engineer at Sibers with no political history. He had brought him in and had Ivan sitting at a table looking at a monitor's live feed of Galina, who questioned him. He was resistant at first. "Didn't want to get anybody in trouble." But eventually, he told her, after assurances, that his daughter, a primary school teacher, had three students in a class of thirty having these "waking dreams," as Galina called them. That was 10 percent of a small social subgroup. She would later run this figure by Yuri, who had studied statistics in college. That was way high but indicative of what, he asked. Galina couldn't answer that yet.

"And they're about events that didn't happen yet but do, like a premonition?" she asked Dorzhiev.

"Yes, most of them, but all inconsequential."

Galina sat back in her chair and added, "For now."

"Thank you, Mr. Dorzhiev. Don't mention this conversation to anybody, especially your daughter. Do you understand me?" Ivan nodded his head.

"You think there's something to this?" he asked with concern.

"If there is, I'll get to the bottom of it one way or the other."

Later she thought about how to approach this investigation. Her section was focused on scientific applications for military or

FSB/SVR development. It had been upgraded after the success of America's DARPA unit with its breakthrough technology over the years. Galina wondered how her superiors would treat her inquiry into "sociological" factors. Their scientific budget was tight and needed to be focused on new weaponry. Her father, a former KGB agent, had warned her about security work, to "don't sit in a puddle" or embarrass yourself with foolish inquiries. But she was part of the new generation, somewhat inspired by Western scientific adventurism or pushing the envelope, as they said. So she would approach it as upgraded "psychic spying." That shouldn't ruffle too many feathers, she hoped.

6

San Francisco, California

Maria was running through a forest with Michael, and they could hear the thrashing about of a large animal chasing them. By the look of the ancient trees and unusual vegetation, the setting was probably prehistoric. Maybe this was a dinosaur stalking them. Michael looked terrified, but then a hangnail would alarm him, Maria thought. The ground started shaking, and she figured the beast was about to pounce on them. An earthquake then opened a deep gorge, and Michael, leading the way, fell into it and was lost. Maria grabbed a hanging vine and swung across the gorge to the other side. She could still hear the echoes of Michael's screams. Across the way, a brachiosaurus from the movie Jurassic Park *came out of the bush. It stood on the edge, bellowing at her.*

Maria woke up in bed with Michael sleeping beside her. She sat up for a moment and then shook him awake. He was groggy and rubbed his eyes.

"Were you having a dream?"

"Yeah, and I got killed again while you got away. So when are you leaving me?"

Maria huffed, "Any day now, handsome. But I want to get in a little more sex beforehand."

"How about right now?"

Maria rolled over in his direction when her cell phone beeped. She counter-rolled, picked it up, and saw the number. "I have to take this."

"Jesus. Tend to your patient while I take a cold shower." They both stood up. Maria walked out of the bedroom and down the stairs to the kitchen with its glowing nightlights. Michael headed for the bathroom, shaking his head and angrily talking to himself.

"How did you like the dinosaur?" Catherine asked.

Maria paused. "But you weren't in the dream."

Cat snorted. "I was the dinosaur."

"Whoa. I'll need to think about that one."

"I mean, is that even possible?"

"We're well beyond that point," Maria added.

She went back to bed but was no longer interested in sex, much to Michael's dismay. He spat out a few grievances, turned on his side, and soon fell asleep. She remained awake. Maria had a few more shared dreams with Catherine Dumont, despite their ongoing biweekly sessions, and often the night of the session like yesterday's, and others with Michael. Since he wasn't in therapy with her, that wasn't countertransference, just unusual. But the shared dreams with Cat weren't personal or compensating for something happening in their lives. Instead, they were archetypal, like what this prehistoric setting suggested. It wasn't about an attitude adjustment but something deeper in the Jungian sense. However, the death dreams with Michael pointed toward a breakup, but Cat sharing tonight's dream was a new facet. Was her bellowing roar a wake-up call? Maria had gone back into analysis with her teacher Evelyn Richardson, who found these shared and waking dreams fascinating but portentous. Something was getting stirred up in the collective unconscious, or so Evelyn sensed.

The next morning Maria rose before Michael, who would no doubt want "a roll in the hay," as he sometimes called morning sex. But she didn't want to dissipate her Eros, which was more than the libido or the sex drive. Wearing his white tennis outfit, red stripes down the shirt and pants, Michael came downstairs as she drank her second cup of coffee. He was in a bad mood and had packed his weekend travel bag. Michael was tall, dark-haired, athletic, and a good tennis player. They were working on her backhand and sometimes played doubles.

He pulled out his car mug and filled it with coffee. "Look, I've got a morning match with Doctor Julian. Think I'll just go home afterward."

"I thought we might go to dinner tonight," Maria said.

"I need a little space. These death and dying dreams are getting to me." Then, before Maria could reply, he added, "And don't give me another analyst take on them."

Maria laughed, trying to break the tension. "Occupational hazard, I'm afraid."

On his way out, Michael passed by her side and kissed Maria on the cheek. "We'll talk about it some other time." He then headed out the door.

She sat there for a long moment. She liked Michael, and they were fairly compatible in a yin-yang sort of way. But did they love each other? This was the real test in any relationship, and it got those couples who did over the bad stretches. She had divorced her first husband, Sean, another psychiatrist. They had everything in common and could talk about interests for days at a time. It took a while for Maria to realize that theirs was more of a companionship than a real in-depth marriage with deeply shared feelings and a physical and emotional attraction. Michael was their financial advisor, and it is why she could afford to live in one of the most expensive neighbors in San Francisco. Their relationship was more basic and primal and what Maria needed as a fallback at the time, but where was the love? And she definitely needed more intellectual stimulation and looked for it elsewhere.

Maria needed to get out of the house today. She grabbed her cell phone and called Catherine. She picked up on the first beep.

"I thought you might call."

"You think." She paused. "You sharing one of my death dreams with Michael is a new element."

"How so?"

Maria thought about her intuition. "I'm wondering if that dinosaur roar wasn't some kind of wake-up call. Maybe I should mend the fence or break it off with him?"

"What would Dr. Richardson say?"

"That your dream presence adds another dynamic element. So, I thought we could take a ride, maybe down Route 1 to Half Moon Bay, and eat lunch there. We need to talk about these dreams out in the real world. Get a different perspective on them."

In her best prudish voice, Cat said, "Is that even allowed, Dr. Jung?"

"Actually, we're crossing a few therapeutic boundaries. Dr. Richardson would say it's drawing outside the lines but would probably agree with this outing. We're already way beyond standard protocol here."

"I'll pick you up and drive us down the coast. It's sunny, and my Mustang is a convertible."

Maria gave her the address.

CATHERINE DROVE UP the winding road of Twin Peaks in central San Francisco to a duplex on a hill with what must have a spectacular ocean view, she assumed. This was the highest residential area in the city and pretty pricey. As she would learn, the woman did love her sunsets. Maria was standing on the porch wearing yellow shorts and a green blouse. She hurried down the steps as Cat drove up.

"No beach bag, Doc?" Cat asked.

"I'm treating this as an on-the-road therapeutic session for both of us." Catherine looked over at her. "You buy lunch."

"Okay, but let's enjoy the ride."

Cat turned the car around, downshifted to a low gear, and headed down the hill, then took 19th street south to Interstate 280 and onto the Route 1 exchange, following it out of town. It was sunny, and they were both wearing sunglasses, but neither talked for a long while.

"You know, I like this, not talking and just cruising along," Cat finally said. "My generation is so busy-busy, talk-talk, to fill up all the empty space."

"Remember. I'm a listener."

"Tell me. I know only too well."

She drove on. They soon left the city as Skyline Drive twisted along the mountainside with its spectacular elevated ocean vista. Its rough and rugged terrain seemed to reflect their dream's setting, if not its lush vegetation. Maria finally asked, "So you were the dinosaur? Exactly, how's that?"

"I don't really know. I just saw you on the other side of the gorge looking across at me, and then I heard this enormous dinosaur roar coming from within me, or so it seemed."

Maria pondered this description, then added, "Remind me not to piss you off."

"Yeah, I'll bite your head off for sure." She saw Maria's look. "One of us is upset about something?"

"At the risk of personal disclosure, I'd say mine's about Michael. We need to figure out yours."

"Maybe Stephanie's allure for me." Catherine paused. "But, Dr. Amidala, if I may, that was one strange dream." She glanced at Maria.

"Yes, it was. Give me a moment."

The road now headed down the mountain to the ocean, and Cat focused on driving it for a while. Finally, they arrived at the beach road, and she headed south at the stoplight. She looked over at Maria. "I mean, have you ever heard anything like that?"

"Frankly, no. But its prehistoric setting is telling."

"Which indicates what?" Cat asked.

"Something very primal and instinctive is trying to make its way into our consciousness."

Cat shook her head. "That sounds scary."

Then, Maria said, in her best analyst voice, "Only if we resist it."

After they passed through Pacifica, the road turned back to the ocean for a half-mile before going inland at Pedro Point. Down from there was the Devil Slide Tunnel with its glaring lights, which offset the mood somewhat but delivered them back to the coast road with its ocean view. Coming from the tunnel into the bright sunlight was jarring, but they soaked up the sun's rays and inhaled the chilled ocean air. It had been a long time since either of them had taken such a drive, and they released themselves to the elements.

At Moss Beach, they took Cabrillo Highway into Half Moon Bay. It was still early, so they started looking for a restaurant to eat breakfast instead of lunch. That's when they passed the sign for the "Dinosaurs of Spanish Town."

"Half Moon Bay was your idea. Is this a setup?" Cat asked.

Maria shook her head. "It's been years since I've come here. I'm sure I knew about this exhibit, but not consciously. It's a synchronicity. Shall we?"

Cat drove into the exhibit of about a dozen red metal sculptures and parked in front of Spanish Town's old craft shop with its window pictures of red rubber dinosaurs for sale. Then, they got out and strolled over to the exhibit, where kids were already roaming among the half-sized dinosaurs with squeals of delight.

"Let's walk around them but check your feeling tone. See if anything comes up," Maria told her. They headed in different directions. After a while, they both ended up in front of the brachiosaurus sculpture from their prehistoric dream. They closed their eyes.

Suddenly, Catherine felt a body shift and found herself in another waking dream, but this time in a prehistoric locale. *Cat felt like she was actually there: the colors were so vibrant, the smell of the plant vegetation intense. She felt so . . . alive. Then, out of the bush, jumped a protohuman woman. They were both startled to see the other and very curious. She stood just over 5-foot-tall, upright with long arms, bare-chested, wearing animal skins over her genitals. She hobbled over to her but not in a hostile way. Put her hands on what must've been Cat's apparition's face and grunted. Then she stepped back, and they just stared at each other. Finally, the woman smiled at her and walked off, waving her into the bush, and Cat could feel the urge to follow her.* Then, she was back in the present and fainted in Maria's arms.

A man rushed over and handed Maria a bottle of water. She splashed Cat's face, and she came around and stood up. Cat then took the bottle and drank it straight down.

"Are you all right?" Maria asked.

Cat scurried away from the exhibit. Maria followed her over to the car.

"Maybe I should drive from here," Maria said.

"You think," Cat snapped, threw her the car keys, walked around to the passenger's side, and slid inside.

"Don't say anything. Let the experience settle in." Maria drove back to the highway and into town, where she found a bar and grill that looked local and rustic. They went inside and took a window-seat booth. An older woman in a light blue waitress outfit brought cups of coffee and menus over without asking. Maria told her they would wait a bit to order. She seemed fine with that.

The two of them just sat there for a long moment before Cat was ready to talk.

"Had a waking dream of a prehistoric era with a protohuman female. Everything was so vivid, the colors, the smells. I mean, she smelled godawful, but I felt more . . . alive than ever. It's hard to describe."

"While the dinosaur sculpture might have triggered it, they were long gone before any protohumans appeared," Maria said,

"I think our dream's prehistoric setting called it up."

"So you popped into her world, or was it a shared waking dream you were both having?"

Catherine closed her eyes. "It was definitely a waking dream but more tactile than the others." She paused, closed her eyes, then opened them. "God. I loved that feeling of being so alive, mentally and emotionally unburdened, and I wanted to follow her into the forest. And she smiled at me, or it looked like that."

Maria shook her head. "Let's put a kibosh on that thought for now." She could've asked if this was related to her friendship with Stephanie Taylor, but that was too analytical for the moment.

The waitress came over, and since Cat was in no shape to read a menu, Maria ordered for them.

Cat was still in a semitrance state and looked out at the road. "You need to pull yourself back," Maria insisted. "Touch things, look at me, Catherine, and eat when the food comes."

She nodded her head. The waitress brought their Western omelets, and they started to eat. Cat was making a real effort to ground herself. Finally, the food and a couple cups of coffee seemed to bring her around. And then she closed her eyes, nodded her head as if she were listening to someone, and popped her eyes wide open in alarm. Cat stood up abruptly, took thirty dollars out of her wallet, and plopped it on the table. "We have to leave. Now!"

Maria stood, waved at the waitress, pointed at the money on the table, and followed Catherine out of the diner. She looked concerned about her patient, then the fire alarm went off, and clouds of black smoke started billowing out of the grill.

Maria got into the Mustang and drove away before getting caught up in the mad rush of cars zooming out of the parking lot. At the highway, she turned north, heading back the way they came. Given the winding roads over the mountains from here to the 280 freeway, this would be the faster route back to her house.

Finally, Cat turned to her. "I saw a little girl with a Russian accent tell me to leave quickly."

"Wow," Maria said. "It sounds like another wake-up call."

"We've got to figure this out, Maria. I mean, I'm in a real panic here. First, the dinosaur dream, and now this. What the hell is happening to me?"

"Remember Jung's *Red Book*?" Maria tentatively asked.

"Yeah. His unconscious upsurges that scared me to death!"

"Calm down, Catherine." The woman made a concerted effort to settle herself. "This seems like those upsurges but more collective. And, as with Jung's, integration is the key to . . ."

"What? My survival?" she spat out.

Maria wondered if it were more than that and then saw images of her other analysands and recalled their complaints about modern life. "Maybe for all of us, and you just crested first, as the surfers say."

Cat looked out at the ocean with its high surf and big waves. "What's today's plan?"

"We drive back to my place. Give you time to ease into it, but later if you're still unsettled, you're staying in my guest room for the night. No driving in this condition."

"Okay. That sounds good."

"But for that to happen, I have to terminate your official therapy. One crossed boundary too many."

"Terminate?" Cat shuddered.

"But not our friendship or ongoing exploration." She gulped a deep breath.

Cat nodded her head. "I understand."

"And we need to talk with Evelyn."

7

London, England

Evelyn sat back in her home office chair and stared at the image on her laptop, placed on an antique Victorian secretary desk. Maria and Catherine Dumont had been sitting in Amidala's home office for some time. She had listened to Maria's reasons for breaking off the woman's formal therapy and agreed that was the best path forward. But, given the circumstances, it didn't break any rules if they continued this "inquiry" as friends. It was early morning here and night there. Evelyn now closed her eyes to digest the extraordinary dream imagery she had just heard.

With her eyes still closed, she asked, "Ms. Dumont, what were you sensing and feeling inside this prehistoric animal."

Catherine and Maria had spent a relaxing afternoon at her house and ate Chinese takeout for dinner. She now closed her eyes and appeared to return to that moment in her shared dream with Maria and Michael. "It's hot, visceral. I have a primal urge to eat and devour everything." She paused. "Instinctual. Almost sexual." She opened her eyes.

Evelyn did the same. "I know this isn't an analytic session, and please forgive me for asking, but what's going on with your sex life."

"Okay, but it's pretty nonexistent right now." She then shared Stephanie's homoerotic offer and its allure to her.

"I see. That's telling. If I may characterize it as such, you intrude into a shared dream of a man and a woman sleeping together days after a woman tried to entice you into a threesome. I believe that's what they call it these days."

Maria reached over and put a hand on Catherine's arm before she overreacted. "I believe Evelyn is pointing out that repressed sexual energy can create such a dream, shared or otherwise."

Evelyn nodded her head. "But, as Jung would say, a woman's sexuality is more spiritual and akin to Eros or relatedness than a man's." She paused. "But what really interests me is the appearance of a protohuman in this waking dream the next day and your urge to follow her into the forest primeval." She paused for a moment and had a thought. "Can you describe her?"

Catherine gave the doctor a general description.

"Her highbrow and upright stature make her closer to the archaic homo sapiens before the evolutionary leap to modern man."

Maria added, "Or the transition from instinctual to mental human."

Catherine took a deep breath. "At that moment, I felt more alive than ever."

"So, Ms. Dumont, on a personal level, it could be urging you to be more instinctual, which comes down to relating to others. It's not telling you or us to regress to that primal state but not to forget our human roots. The lack you feel is a lack of relatedness that is pervasive in this age of diminished Eros, in its classical or Platonic sense."

Catherine looked at Maria. "So don't beat yourself up because you're not in a personal relationship; everybody feels this lack of relatedness at some level."

Evelyn added, "Before we get to this other waking dream, I could add that you might consider this Taylor woman's offer, given the prehistoric woman beckoning you."

Maria almost gasped at this suggestion. "Evelyn. Really."

"We're just friends here trying to give each other our advice."

Everybody sat back in their chairs and let this exchange settle. Then, finally, Evelyn picked up the thread. "And then, moments after you have this primeval waking dream, a little Russian girl intrudes into your life in another WD, if I may call it that, to save you from a life-threatening explosion."

Maria nodded her head. "Are you saying that Catherine's earlier call to life is being protected by a collective unconscious response?"

"Precisely," Evelyn added, "which seems to be directing this particular waking dream state."

"It's pretty global if it's coming from Russia halfway across the planet," Maria added.

"And this euphoric feeling at the woman beckoning me?" Catherine asked.

"A catharsis, typically the sense of relief at resolving an unconscious conflict. From the Greek *katharsis*, purification," Evelyn added.

Maria said, "And if this diner episode were a nighttime dream, the explosion might tell you that you're taking a critical situation too lightly."

"Or, from a collective point of view, which seems to be the thrust of these episodes, we all need to prepare for a collective explosive situation," Evelyn said.

"Whoa." Catherine stood up, walked over to the room's mini-fridge, and took out a bottle of water." She could hear Maria say from across the room, "Shake it off, Cat." She did and, most dramatically, then walked over to the office desk and its laptop screen.

"Are you feeling any better?" Evelyn asked with genuine concern.

"Yes, and I think I can drive home now and let the two of you carry on with it."

"Are you sure?" Maria asked.

"What did Jung once say, 'The unconscious just wants to be acknowledged?' Message received."

Maria nodded her head. "Yes, and thus made conscious, I might add." She turned to Evelyn on her laptop screen. "Give me a moment. I'll walk Cat out to her car." Her teacher and analyst nodded her head. Maria stood up.

"That's okay. I'm fine and just want to hurry off."

"All right." They stood there for a long moment, not knowing if they should hug. Then, finally, Catherine nodded, turned, and walked out of the room and down the stairs.

Maria sat at her desk and took a deep breath. "Wow, it's been an eventful twenty-four hours."

Evelyn shook her head. "Get used to it. I sense these episodes are just the beginning, and that young lady seems to be the center of it all."

"Yes, but the center of what?" Maria asked.

"Shall we?"

They now began to explore what these shared and waking dreams might mean for humanity's collective welfare in deeper Jungian and psychological terms. There wasn't much to go on. Richardson only had one analysand having had a "waking dream," and Maria, Catherine, and Michael were the only ones having multiple shared dreams in their recent experience. But looking back at humankind's progress through the centuries, there were collective leaps in consciousness where an outmoded state of religion or culture needed an infusion of new energy to free the human spirit.

Were these waking dream states the presage of such a movement from the Collective Unconscious?

Hours later, and not much further along in their understanding of the global situation, Maria's phone chimed. It was Catherine. She immediately picked it up. "Are you all right?"

"Yes. Still online with Dr. Richardson?"

"We're just getting ready to break it off."

"Tell her that I got home and took her advice about that offer, and it was liberating." They all laughed exuberantly.

Later, Catherine had a shared dream with Jeff and Stephanie, and it felt like she was ready for what would come next.

EVELYN WAS IN HER UNIVERSITY OFFICE between classes two days later with piles of dusty books and blue test folders stacked high. She made her students write it out, not type it out. Her secretary buzzed her. "A Mr. Harris is on the line, no first name or company."

"Tell him I'm not here."

A moment later, she called her back. "He says that's fine. He'll have the constable drag you out of your office."

Evelyn picked up the phone. "What's this about, Harris?"

"Look, Richardson, I'll just say what you told Officer Davies has created a real shitstorm with us and MI6, and we need to get some clarification."

"I have a class to teach, and you can't compel me to cooperate with you."

"Under the National Security Act, I can compel citizens to cooperate with us or face jail time."

"All this over Makarov's wet dream about the Russian President?"

"I'll discuss that with you at headquarters. Davies and a constable will be there shortly."

Evelyn slammed the phone down. She buzzed her secretary. "Millie, get Everette to teach my Four O'clock. I've been called away."

The two men showed up in ten minutes and escorted her to the constable's Austin Metro police car. They arrived at the Thames House in Millbank twenty minutes later. Dr. Richardson was taken to an interrogation room. She declined an offer of coffee or water, and waited thirty minutes before Gerald Harris, mid-sixties, gray-haired but fit for his age, stepped inside. He sat down and slipped on his dark-colored reading glasses.

"Sorry about the room Richardson and the wait, but some of the higher-ups here and in the foreign service want to monitor our talk." He nodded to the two-way window.

"Okay, let's get on with it. I don't have all day."

He opened a folder and read through a report, then looked up. "You told Officer Davies that your patient, the Russian Fyodor Makarov, who we can't locate, had a 'waking dream' of Vladimir Putin in his office, telling a crony that he would create a crisis to keep him in office. Is that correct?"

"Yes. And Makarov told this waking dream to his fellow dissidents, and I was afraid it would get back to the Russians, and he needed protection."

"A waking dream. Can you explain that?"

"It's like a daydream but of actual events."

"How is that possible?" Harris asked, leaning over the table.

"It's my first encounter with it. I mean, everybody has fantasy daydreams, but not of something this specific and apparently prophetic."

"I find this hard to believe. Maybe Makarov was just putting you on. Dr. Hardgrave said he compelled him to see you."

"Okay, maybe he did. He's a crusty old fart. So are we finished here?"

Harris sat back in his chair. "Let's say it actually happened. Do you think they occur often, or is this just a one-time aberration?"

"He only reported one other waking dream about an old girl-friend. None of my other analysands, or those seeing other analysts in my group, have ever reported them," she said, not mentioning Maria's Catherine Dumont.

"Could this be something like what the Americans used to call remote viewing?"

"I'm familiar with that research, and it appears to be something similar but spontaneous without all the protocols they used, maybe even telepathy."

Harris leaned forward. "You can see why an intelligence agency would be interested in this . . . phenomenon."

"In my opinion, it's not something that you can develop and use, and in this case, it was very specific to somebody with a con-nection to the subject."

"Okay, but this subject is of great interest to the Americans and us these days. When we find Makarov, and we will find him, would you be willing to work with him? We'd like to see if he can call up more of these . . . waking dreams."

"Absolutely not. I'm a psychiatrist, not one of your shitbird handlers, and I've only shared this with you to protect my patient. There are laws that protect the sanctity of the doctor-patient rela-tionship."

Harris shook his head. "In the case of national security, they don't apply, and we can compel you to work with us or lose your license."

"I'll see what my lawyer and the British Psychological Society, with its 60,000 members, say about that."

Harris shook his head and stood up. "You can go now, but we'll be in touch." He stepped toward the door, then turned around. "Oh, and what we discussed here is top secret, and you can't share it with anybody."

"I have a right to share my therapeutic insights with colleagues, and you can't just slap that top-secret tag on my sessions with analysands."

"Yeah, test me."

"I will. You can count on it."

An apologetic Ronald Davies drove Evelyn back to London University. She answered a few emails, picked up her briefcase, and walked home. Evelyn was amazed by how this waking dream phenomenon had suddenly blown up in her face. When she arrived there, she called Edward Henry of the BPS at home. They have been colleagues for thirty years. She told him about the waking dreams some analysands were having, something new on the horizon, and how MI5 wanted to exploit them.

Henry said, "This Harris guy is just trying to intimidate you, Evelyn. We have a committee that looks into such coercive tactics by the government. There are no legal statutes that could compel you to work with them or stop you from investigating this phenomenon."

"That sounds reassuring, Edward. I did work for them briefly in the 1980s and signed agreements back then, but I would think nothing that could affect my practice today."

"The government doesn't have a right to interfere or restrict your therapeutic practice, and they'll have to jail all of us if they try."

"Let's hope it doesn't come to that."

WHEN HARRIS RETURNED to his office after a debriefing with his division head, he pulled out Richardson's MI5 file from the late 1980s. He was a rookie back then, working with Jason Lewis on Russian dissidents. While MI6 recruited dissidents, once in England, MI5 worked with the foreign service, somewhat like the America FBI and the CIA, to monitor their activities. And when they broke Yuri Yegorov, it was a breakthrough career-making case for them. Lewis got promoted to division head, and Harris was assigned to Richardson to continue "uncovering double agents," as he was told. When the psychiatrist refused to continue working with them, despite his heavy-handed importune to her, it almost ruined his career. It took years to recover from this blow. And now, this new development, some kind of psychic link to Vladimir Putin, could keep him relevant and off the retirement list. Richardson owed him as much, and he would clamp down on her to get his due.

Officer Davies now stuck his head through the cracked door. A thin, pale-faced young man, he appeared too shy for this kind of security work, but Harris learned early on that he was brilliant and efficient, with no personality quirks.

Harris looked up. "Did the old crone have anything to say?"

Davies took a seat. "No, not really. Other than her claims of client confidentiality."

"And what's your take on Makarov's waking dream ingress?"

"I'll need to research it, but from watching your interview with her, I'd say it's real, if unknown, and we need to pursue it further."

"Good. And Ron, the gloves come off with this bitch. She almost ruined my career before it even got started. I have some 'evening up' to do with her."

Davies cringed a bit. "Yes, sir."

8

Novosibirsk, Russia

Her teacher Arina Dorzhiev had told Elena to lie to the woman from Moscow. No, she only saw her teacher's car accident and little Dimitri getting hit by the volleyball. Nothing else. The woman kept asking her questions but to no avail. She then assembled the whole school in the gymnasium and asked if anybody had these waking dreams besides Elena. Only two other students raised their hands, Gregor and Katya, again. She seemed rather disappointed when she left and flew back to Moscow. After school that day, Ms. Dorzhiev drove her home.

"I know you don't like to lie, Elena. It's not what your parents taught you, but sometimes we must keep our inner life private. Do you understand?"

"But can I tell you, Ms. Dorzhiev?"

"Yes, but only outside of school." Arina looked over at the little blond ten-year-old.

"I see people, foreign people, and some about to have . . . accidents, and I tell them."

"Does this happen very often?" Arina asked.

"Only a couple of times, but only people I feel . . . connected to somehow."

"That's good, Elena. We need to help people when we can, but don't tell anybody else about that, not your parents or even your brother."

"Why not?" she asked.

"People are afraid of things not part of their normal lives or possibilities."

The girl nodded.

Her teacher paused. "Elena, does anybody come to you in what we're calling a waking dream?"

Elena thought about that and then shook her head. Maybe it was best not to tell even Ms. Dorzhiev about David. Her teacher dropped her off at the bus stop and told her to wait until the bus came before walking home. None of the kids asked how she got here before them. They were trained not to ask each other such questions by their parents, some of whom still remembered, as they said, the "old days."

That night Elena went to her room at eight o'clock, lay down, and called out to David in America. He was walking to school, and she appeared to him and said not to tell anybody about them talking to each other. He understood and told her about the psychologist who had come to his school and asked about him seeing the little boy fall off the slide. Elena told him about the female officer who had asked her similar questions. They could communicate in what looked like a computer window, similar to her brother's conversations on Facebook. David said he had tried to contact the boy who fell off the slide, but the boy was afraid and didn't respond. Once they had one of these daydreams, they could sometimes tune into the other person and "talk," but not always.

After talking with David, Elena felt energized and went to her brother Nikolay's room. As always at night, he was on Facebook and video-chatting with girls in other cities. She didn't disturb him and just watched from the back of the room. Suddenly, Elena had a waking dream of the girl on Nikolay's screen. She was now in her room and could see her brother on the video screen. Suddenly, the girl sensed somebody was there, maybe her father, and abruptly turned off her computer. She swiveled around in her chair and was surprised to see Elena's blurry image. The girl had black hair with red stripes and purple lipstick.

"Who are you, little girl?" she asked.

"Just someone looking in on you."

"This is very interesting." She reached out to touch her but saw that the girl was only an apparition.

"What's your name?" Elena asked.

"I'm Inna Kuzmin, and you are?"

Elena thought about telling her the truth but said, "Masha," instead.

"How are we doing this without a computer?"

"My friend David says it's like a daydream."

The girl laughed. "This is better than Facebook. Can you teach me how to do this?"

"But only if you're a good person."

The girl narrowed her eyes. "I try, but I . . . fail sometimes." Inna took a deep breath. "This feels really good."

Elena nodded her head. "Try harder, and I'll be back, but don't tell any-body about our 'friending' each other."

Elena was back in Nikolay's room, and Inna suddenly appeared on her brother's computer screen.

"What happened? We lost our connection," he asked Inna.

"Something extraordinary . . ." she stopped, closed her eyes, and exhaled a deep breath. "The computer just turned itself off. I had to reboot."

Elena smiled; Inna was actually glowing. She needed to get one of these computers to connect with more people around the world. Maybe she could talk with David in America on Facebook and hunt for other dreamers. So she went looking for her father, Viktor. He was in his home office studying financial websites on his laptop. Elena asked what he was doing, and he told her he was figuring out what stocks to buy and explained what they were. Suddenly, Elena had a waking dream, or how she related to it, and saw one of these companies, Yandex, soaring in its ratings over the next year. She stepped forward and pointed to it on her father's list of companies.

"That's the one to buy. The internet company."

Her father smirked. "Oh, really. Why's that my little financial genius?" Her father now called up the company's profile and nodded his head after a while.

"Young people are looking for answers and don't trust what they hear in school or what the TV news or newspapers say."

"For us adults, too," her father added.

"I know, daddy." She paused. "If you make money off it, will you buy me a computer like Nikolay's?"

"Aren't you a little young for that?"

"No. Things are speeding up, and little kids grow up faster now."

His father nodded his head. "I can see that. Maybe next year for your birthday."

Elena turned to walk out of his office but stopped and looked back. She watched her father buy the Yandex stock. Good. She went to her room and lay on the bed. Elena wondered what the woman in California was doing but was too tired to check on her. She needed to rest up for her nighttime dreaming adventures.

Dayton, Ohio

David felt charged up at school that day. Talking with the Russian girl did that, and he liked the feeling it brought but would hide its expression from others. David also kept a watchful eye today at school. Whenever Elena showed up, he was prone to have another waking dream, as the woman from back East called it. But nothing like that happened at school, and he took the bus to their suburban home northeast of town.

That night his father had Air Force friends over for dinner. One of them was a new pilot the other men had taken "under their wing," as his father told him. First Lieutenant Jordan Merriweather had been flying jets at the airbase for the last year and working his way up the rotation, as they say. This was a special dinner, and his mother, Joyce, fixed steaks and baked potatoes, one of David's favorite meals. After dinner, but before the men retired to his father's game room with its big-screen TV where they planned to watch *Monday Night Football*, David looked at this airman with brown squinty eyes and had another waking dream. He saw the dark-haired man in a jet developing problems. Back at the table, the airman looked at him as if he sensed something odd.

David spoke up as the men were drinking their coffees. He looked to Lieutenant Merriweather. "Sir, are you going to fly tomorrow?"

"Yes. I'm taking a spin on an F-35. My first time. It's one of the best combat jets in the Air Force. Why do you ask, son?"

"I'm just wondering if you wear parachutes when you fly?"

"Yes, and we have ejection seats that clear us from the plane." Jordan could see the boy's concern. "Don't worry. Flying jets is safer than driving cars on the freeway around here."

"Ain't that the truth," one of the pilots added.

The others nodded their heads and laughed off the boy's concern. His father narrowed his eyes, then turned to the men. "Okay, guys. Ready for some football."

As they left the dinner table, Mark looked over at Joyce and nodded at their son. David helped his mother clear the table and put the dishes in the dishwasher. While they worked, his mother asked, "David, what was that about? Asking Lieutenant Merriweather if he wore a parachute."

Taking Elena's advice, he didn't say anything about his waking dream. He didn't like to lie to his parents, but he sensed that he couldn't reveal too much about what he was experiencing.

"Oh, nothing. He just seems so young to be flying big jets, that's all."

His mother nodded her head. "You're right about that. I hope you don't follow in your father's footsteps."

"Me too," David said. Afterward, he went back to his room and played a video game. He could hear his father and the pilots whooping it up in the game room downstairs. David was tempted to contact Elena and tell her what had happened, but he didn't like having these daydreams close together.

When he got back from school the following day, his father was home early from work. He was sitting on the sofa with his mother. David sensed that something was wrong or that he was in trouble.

"David, come over and have a seat," his father said.

He walked to the padded chair across from the sofa and sat down. "Is something wrong?"

"David, Lieutenant Merriweather had a . . . problem with his jet today, but he was able to bring it in. We know you had that dream thing with the little boy who fell off the sliding board in Springfield. And given your questions after dinner last night, we wondered if you saw something like that happening with the Lieutenant?"

David nodded his head but didn't speak.

"What did you see, David?"

"I saw him in the jet's cockpit; it was shaking, and he was flipping switches on the . . . I've heard you call it the yoke, and talking excitedly on the radio. Then he smiled at me like I was there. And he just calmed down and took care of it. I felt better, too." Actually, these daydreams left him feeling "connected," as Elena said.

His father just shook his head. That last detail didn't compute, as he would say, so he dismissed it. "Thankfully, he's all right, and you didn't do anything wrong, David. We just need to understand these . . . waking dreams—I believe Ms. Holmes called them—that you're having."

"Is she coming back to talk with me? I liked her."

"Yes, David. You're staying home from school tomorrow, and she'll talk with you here."

"Okay."

His mother now said. "David. Wash up, and you can help me in the kitchen. I'm cooking spaghetti and meatballs."

"That's great, mom."

The following morning David was in the game room watching cartoons on the big-screen TV when his mother brought in Ms. Holmes. The woman sat on the couch next to him, and his mother set a tray of tea, drinks, and cookies on the coffee table.

"I'll leave the two of you alone."

The woman had a few inquiries about how things were going at school, his interests, and what he did with his friends on weekends. Then they talked about what she called his waking dream and the jet pilot's episode. David described it as he had to his parents. Ms.

Holmes asked if he had had other episodes since they last talked. David told her this was the only other one like that.

"David. You shouldn't be concerned. This occurrence is something new that we're exploring as school psychologists. Other children are reporting similar episodes. But we've also gotten reports like what you told me about the little girl who stopped you from crossing the street. Do you remember that?"

David nodded but was reluctant to say more about it, given his ongoing relationship with Elena and their special friendship.

"Let's explore that some more. You said the girl just shook her head at that time." David nodded. "She didn't speak?"

"No."

"And you've never seen this girl again?" David shook his head but looked down. He felt terrible about lying to her, but he knew that Elena was right. They have to be careful with adults, despite their concerns for them.

Alicia now opened the folder she had set on the table and slid over the artist's rendering of this girl from her last visit and a grainy black-and-white photo of Elena.

"David, is this a photo of the girl you saw who warned you about the reckless driver?"

He couldn't deny that and nodded his head. "Yes, that's her. How did you get her photo?"

Alicia put the material back in her folder. "Her name is Elena Mongush, and she lives in western Russia. And David, if she ever contacts you again, you must have your parents call me immediately."

"Yes, ma'am."

After Ms. Holmes left and while his mother was busy in the kitchen, David tried to contact Elena in Russia. The girl was asleep but soon appeared in his game room in her dreaming body.

"How are you doing this?" David asked.

"I'm sleeping, so I think this is my spirit body, as Mom says."

"A psychologist showed me a picture of you, and I had to tell her it was you who looked in on me."

"That's all right, David. But we have to be careful. Adults don't understand yet, but they will. Our energy will open them up."

"Oh, that's good to know. I don't like lying to my parents."

"My teacher, Arina, told me that sometimes we should keep our inner experiences to ourselves." She paused. "Will you help me reach out to others, David?" Elena asked.

"I've been afraid to, but saving the pilot made me feel really good, like I mattered. I know we need others to help spread this."

"Only if it feels right?" David nodded his head. "And, if you take a nap now, we can share our dreamtime."

"Okay. Wait for me."

Elena's image disappeared. David got up and walked into the kitchen. "Mom, I'm tired. I think I'll take a nap."

"That's good, David. I'll fix lunch when you wake up."

David nodded. He couldn't wait to dream with Elena.

9

Arlington, Virginia

DARPA Director Charlotte Blackman sat at a round table in her office with General Morton and his two SPS scientists, Greg Mires and Alicia Holmes. First, she examined the artist's drawing and the black-and-white photo of the little girl from Siberia, Russia. Then, she looked across at Alicia. "And Major Bernard's son had one of these waking dreams with her that warned him about a reckless driver?"

"Yes, ma'am. David said that this Elena Mongush was the girl he had seen, but I believe he lied to me about further contact with her."

Blackman turned to General Morton. "And MI6's mole at the FSB is where you got the girl's photo and name?"

"Yes, Galina Ilyin, their emerging science officer, went to the girl's school in Novosibirsk and discovered that two other children there were having these . . . episodes in her class of 30."

Blackman raised an eyebrow. "That's off the chart. Psychic contagion?"

"Yes, and as the report goes on to say, she believed that Elena was lying about having other episodes, possibly coached by her teacher, Arina Dorzhiev. This city is where Russia used to conduct their parapsychology experiments back in the 1960s and 70s."

Blackman picked up the photo of Russian dissident Fyodor Makarov. "And this Russian dissident told his psychiatrist that he saw Vladimir Putin in his Kremlin office discussing top-secret plans?"

Morton nodded his head. "About creating a crisis to keep him in office, and then there were these recent troop movements on the Ukraine border."

She sat back in her chair and looked over at Morton. "Well, Stanley, you certainly have a hot potato here. So what's the concern? The Russians will develop child psychics to spy on us?" she chortled.

Morton pushed a report across the table to her. "This is a transcript of MI5's interrogation of Makarov's psychiatrist, Dr. Richardson, an old but uncooperative asset from the 80s. She claims that while what he saw was like those old remote-viewing visions, they're spontaneous and can't be focused on targets like with that protocol. They then ran this opinion by their psyche experts, and they agreed, as did ours."

"Okay, and it's like your child genius example when we first talked. So you think these waking dreams, or whatever they are, might spread in the population and become a social and global threat?"

Morton looked to Dr. Mires. He added, "Yes, a threat, but to whom: themselves, governments, and private security firms, or to those . . . left behind in what might be an evolutionary leap?"

Blackman asked, "Watch a lot of sci-fi, do we, Dr. Mires?" Greg laughed. "It's far too early to make such claims."

"Our job is to look for possible Black Swans. If millions, possibly tens of millions, globally start having these waking dreams, and at some point learn to control them . . ."

Blackman nodded her head. "I agree that could get dicey." She turned to General Morton. "And what do you want from DARPA?"

"My boss at the DOD told me to inform you of this development in case we may need to draw on your resources at some point."

"Okay. I agree. If you like, I could fold you into one of our programs and get you more funding."

General Morton stood, and the others followed. "Charlotte. I want to keep our independence for now."

She stood and shook hands with the General. "I understand."

Back in the SPS offices, the General held a group meeting. "Didn't want to bring this up with Blackman, she's a pretty straight arrow, but my contacts at the NSA have added 'waking dreams' to their keyword internet and telecommunication monitoring worldwide." He paused and looked around the table. "Anybody got a problem with that?" Nobody objected.

Greg added, "Have their results piped into Emily's secure server."

Morton nodded his head. "Team. This is our Black Swan. Why we were sanctioned. Yes, Blackman's right; it's far too early to 'jump the gun,' as it were. But that's the nature of Black Swan events; they appear out of nowhere like the impact of the Global Internet, and then before you know, they 'eat your lunch.'" This idiom got smiles from the group.

"From now on, it's our sole focus. MI5 is monitoring Evelyn Richardson, and they've reported that Dr. Maria Amidala, a psychiatrist in San Francisco and a former student, first brought this phenomenon to her attention. I have a National Security Directive that will allow the NSA to monitor her communications and anybody else having these episodes, especially her patients. At some point, we will want to find a daydreamer, I guess you could call them, who will cooperate with us to test the parameters of this dreaming state. So let's find somebody. The Bernard boy is too young. We want an adult or at least a teenager."

Morton stood up. "Guess I don't need to say it, but I will. This has a Top Secret classification. Do not share any of it with anybody outside this office, including DARPA employees. If you need to bring somebody into the loop, have Greg contact me for authorization."

The General left, and the others just sat there in shock. Eric Darby looked around the table. He then reached into his pants pocket and took out a blue vitamin pill. "Anybody want to take the blue pill?"

There was a brief moment before everybody started laughing, hooting, and slapping the table. "Eric, you're the best," Emily roared and threw him a kiss.

Greg recovered first. "We've already taken Morpheus's red pill when we signed up, but I'll have to admit I didn't think it would go this far this fast."

Eric asked, "Do you think they've bugged our office?"

"Look, guys," Greg said, "We all signed nondisclosure agreements to walk in here. So don't get paranoid, and just do your job."

Everybody went back to their offices. Alicia followed Greg to his and sat across the desk from him. "What do you want to do about David Bernard? I'm almost sure he's having more of these episodes with this Elena girl in Russia."

"The good thing is that he has cooperative parents. Didn't you ask them to keep you appraised if he talks about any other dreams?"

"Yes, but I feel his contact with Elena is almost sacred to him. I think my questioning alerted him and that the two of them will be more careful about future disclosures."

Greg shook his head. "Look, I don't want to go after kids. First, we need to know more about this phenomenon."

"Since Richardson and her student Amidala are both Jungians, I'll go back and study his work a little more thoroughly. I know

84

a professor at The C.G. Jung Institute of Chicago. I took under-graduate courses with him there."

"So you drop in and talk to him about waking dreams? Won't he be curious? Want to know your interest in this subject?"

"I have a cover identity as a journalist backstopped with pub-lished articles."

There was a knock on the door, and Emily stuck her head inside. Greg waved her over, and she stepped up to his desk. "Our cup runneth over. The British Psychological Society posted a notice in their journal going out to 60,000 members asking if anyone was dealing with waking dreams."

"Good. Can you hack their system and monitor the replies?" Greg asked.

"I did, and we're not the only ones spying on them."

"Ah, our British friends." He paused. "Just don't step on their toes."

Emily squinted her eyes. "Not unless they step on mine."

San Francisco, California

Catherine was driving across the Golden Gate Bridge on her way to work. It was sunny and clear, and she had the Mustang's top down to let the ocean breeze blow over her. Suddenly, Cat had a waking dream, but not as distracting as the last one here; it was more like a screen opened up, and the little Russian girl appeared. She told her that the military had found out about us and was "listening in." Then she was gone. Afterward, she felt the same energy shift. This had happened with the other episodes but was getting more intense. This outreach was progressing rapidly, as were her contact skills.

Catherine's ad agency was located downtown and not far from Amidala's building. When she arrived at her office, Cat turned on her computer and called Maria after looking at today's work schedule. She had waited to call at the top of the hour to catch her between patients. She suggested that they have lunch together; Maria hesitated but named a restaurant and would meet her there. Instead, Cat said she would pick her up and wanted to go elsewhere. The urgent tone of her friend's voice told her that this was more than a casual get-together.

Catherine spent the morning focusing on one of the agency's new clients. They were an international clothing retailer hit hard by last year's COVID shutdown and needed a new logo for their business. This California sportswear company had stores across the country, and its line was picked up in foreign clothing stores worldwide. People were now coming out of their shells and going into the world again and needed more exercise. So Catherine designed a logo, a colorful circle with slices of people: jogging, playing tennis, hiking, and swimming. The owners had approved the design but wanted it less busy, so she toned down the background and simplified the images on each slice that punched out the activities. She emailed it to their creative director, who raved about it, and sent it to the client.

Catherine picked Maria up at 12:30 and said she was taking her to a new seafood place. It was across town, and they took a cab there. They only exchanged pleasantries in the cab, which again piqued Maria's concern. Finally, seated at a bay-vista window table, Cat explained herself.

"I had another waking dream driving on the Golden Gate today. It was the little Russian girl. She told me that the government knew about us and that they were 'listening in.'"

"About us?" Maria asked.

"I felt she was talking about people having these shared and waking dreams."

Maria sighed. "I guess it was only a matter of time." She paused and thought about it. "Look, I have an analysand, a Silicon Valley techy who could probably set us up with high-grade encryption apps—I think they call them—on our cell phones."

"Also, get him to tell you about an off-the-shelf camera and bug detectors."

"Couldn't you just get that online from Amazon?" Maria asked.

"Yes, but you'd leave a paper trail. Buying it with cash at an electronics store is safer."

Maria sat back in her chair. The waitress came over with menus, and they both ordered iced teas as their beverage. After she left, "You've given this some thought."

"At work, our offices and phones are scanned for bugs every six months."

"Really, in advertising?"

"It's a cutthroat business when you get at our level, and with the business slowdown, agencies and their clients are getting desperate."

Their iced teas came. They ordered, took sips of their teas, and looked out the window at the Bay with the seagulls gliding along the thermal air currents.

"The girl spoke to you in English?"

"Yes, like before and with an accent, but I had the feeling that however this works, the collective mind translates it." She paused. "And maybe, like with this little girl, stimulates our functions like intelligence."

"I'll run all this by Evelyn, but since MI5 has already brought her in for questioning, she's probably figured out they're spying on us."

"But it tells us this is far more pervasive than we thought, that they're detecting it in people worldwide," Cat added.

Maria said, "Think of how fast the COVID virus spread globally. It's not nearly the same thing, but in this case, the 'psychic virus' doesn't even need physical contact."

"No, but not everybody contacted would be a willing carrier if I can extend the metaphor," Cat added.

"Yes. But I can imagine the government's concern, given Evelyn's Russian dissident listening in on a Kremlin meeting, that these waking dreams could be another form of ESP or remote viewing to spy on them."

Cat had a thought. "And it's not a communication medium they can hack or bug."

"So it's a control issue for them, and why they've jumped on it so fast?"

Maria now opened her purse and pulled out this month's BPS journal. She had marked the notice on page 5 and handed it to Catherine.

She read the waking dream inquiry and looked up. "This goes out worldwide?"

"Yes, to 60,000 members. I mean, Carl Jung was a charter member back in the 1950s. But this will probably get some media attention as well, so the proverbial cat is out of the bag."

Catherine laughed. "Will give delusional patients everywhere a real boost."

Maria nodded her head. "As well as my business. It'll just be separating the wheat from the chaff."

Their meals came. They had both ordered linguini with clam sauce, Maria's with red sauce, and Cat's with white. They ate a few bites and let the food and their concerns settle. The Bay was choppy today, and Catherine looked out at it.

Maria shook her head. "I can see the government's concern. But something much more vital is happening here at a collective unconscious level. The self-contained barriers of our psyches might be breaking down, and that could presage a troubling upheaval for many." She paused. "Or before we find another common ground."

Cat sat back in her chair. Then, suddenly, something dawned on her. "Oh, my God. I remember my father going on and on about this defrocked French priest, Pierre Teilhard de Chardin, preaching how we're all going to come together into one unified psychic whole or consciousness."

Maria nodded her head. "Yes, I've had analysands cite him."

"Really?" Cat asked in surprise.

"New Agers from Marin County needing psychiatric help," Maria added.

Catherine laughed. "Don't we all."

"Well, some just need a push in the right direction."

"Like over the side of a cliff."

"'Until you spread your wings, you'll have no idea how far you can fly,' to quote Napoleon of all people."

They clinked their water glasses.

10

San Rafael, California

Stephanie Taylor drove up Highway 101, heading for her exit north of the city. Her boyfriend, Jeff Seymour, had wanted her to come home with him to Mill Valley after dinner in San Francisco. He had attended a fashion show where she was one of the featured models, but she didn't want to follow him home. After this gala, which was all about bodies and their expression as much as the clothes, she felt different. This feeling baffled her; in the past, dinner out with him was usually their entrée to all-night sex. But when Catherine entered the equation, it had shifted that appetite for her. She didn't want to make love to Jeff tonight but connect to Cat. The woman had only joined them twice, but it changed things. Yes, some models were bisexual, and she had had a few flings in that regard. But this was something else, and it disturbed her. Finally, she exited the 101 and drove up to her mountainside home.

She got out of her BMW carrying a bag full of show mementos showered on the models. Stephanie dropped the bag in the trash can as she headed up the steep walkway to the front door. Inside, she immediately stripped off the gold lamé loaner dress she had modeled at the show and left it on the floor. Jeff had insisted she wear it to their dinner at Saison, where he practically put her on display. At one point, she told him, "Why don't I just straddle you here at the table." He took her seriously.

"I could follow you to the bathroom, and we could do it in a stall."

Stephanie just shook her head and ordered another glass of champagne. Later, when she needed to go to the lady's room, she gave him a sit-tight look, just in case. Jeff could be so literal-minded.

At home she took a shower, subconsciously trying to wash off all the amorous male vibes directed at her this evening. After tonight's show, she decided to do only photoshoots in the future. Stephanie dried herself off, slipped into a nightgown, and then between the silky sheets of her bed. She sat up and read a chapter from a religious book an Indian hairdresser had given her recently at a show in New Delhi. Stephanie didn't quite understand the poetry of this ancient Hindu text, but it always seemed to restore her.

Then she heard, "Steph, look up."

She put her book down and saw a blurry image of Catherine standing at the foot of her bed. This must be a dream, she thought, but I'm awake. Stephanie rubbed her eyes, but her friend was still standing there.

"Holy shit. How did you get in here, Cat?"

"I'm not really here, Steph. This is what's called a waking dream."

Stephanie slipped out of bed, walked around, and sat at the end of the bed. She reached out to touch Catherine, but her hand went through her.

"So you're a ghost or something?"

"No, I believe my mother would call it my astral body." Cat stepped over, sat next to her, and then wrapped her etheric arms around Stephanie. The woman gasped.

"Well, I can feel that, and it feels extraordinary."

"Go back to bed, Steph, and I'll lie next to you, but don't get sexual with me right now, or I'll get pulled away."

Stephanie did as instructed, and she lay next to her disembodied lover and fell asleep. She then had the most wonderful dream and connected deeply with Catherine, drawing in this white light surrounding her. Stephanie had never related to anyone in her life this way or in her adult life. She could now remember doing this kind of active dreaming with girlfriends as a child but had long forgotten those episodes.

It was late when she woke up in the morning, but she felt energized. She stood up, walked over to the picture-glass window, and pulled aside the drapes. Stephanie looked out at the mountains to the east with the sun shining overhead. Another glorious California day. She went to her dresser, opened her wallet, and pulled out her friend's business card. Stephanie picked up her cell phone and went down the stairs to the kitchen, where she turned on her already-prepped coffeemaker and called Catherine.

"Catherine, this is Stephanie Taylor."

"Oh, so you remember last night."

"Oh, Jesus. That was for real. It's hard to believe. Can I drive in and have lunch with you? We need to talk."

"It's a little late for lunch, given your drive time, Steph. How about dinner, someplace private where no one will recognize you?"

"Yes. I know just the place."

"Okay, text me, and Steph, dress down. We don't want to call attention to you."

The Italian bistro was located in the same general vicinity of the Ritz Carlton, where her agency kept a room for out-of-town models. She called and reserved it, just in case, and then felt something shift in her. This get-together wasn't about that kind of craving but another.

Stephanie showed up wearing a gray-patterned bucket hat to cover her luxurious blond hair and a woman's pantsuit to hide the rest of her. She had made reservations under an alias used for such occasions. They seated her as requested in the back of the restaurant. Minutes later, Catherine showed up and was taken back to her.

Stephanie smiled as Cat sat down, then reached over and touched her hand. "Want to make sure it's you in the flesh."

"Hope I didn't frighten you last night, but I guess it was time for us to . . . connect this way."

She thought of responding with a flirty rejoinder but stopped herself. How interesting. The waitress brought over menus, and they ordered a bottle of Sauvignon Blanc, which she served, and they sat back and took their first sips.

"Okay, Cat. Why don't you tell me what's up? I've got a feeling this isn't just about us and our attraction for each other."

Catherine gave a rundown of what had been happening to her, the work with Dr. Amidala, the worldwide spread of these waking and shared dreaming states, and maybe its importance for humanity.

"Wow. That's a lot to digest. Our shared dream last night did awaken memories of something similar as a child before the sexual abuse." This recall brought something up. She closed her eyes, felt her way through it, and released a breath. Stephanie opened her eyes.

Catherine reached over and took her hand. "I'm sorry to hear about the abuse." She sat back for a moment and looked the model in the eye. "Since this seems to have started with a ten-year-old girl in Russia, we think it might have something to do with us reclaiming the innocence of childhood. That is, before all our conditioning set in, as Maria says, when we were more at one with all-there-is, as my father would say." She paused. "I can't believe I'm quoting Barry again."

"What was your relationship with him?" Stephanie tentatively asked.

"Since most teenagers think their parents are crazy, I thought as much, but this experience is revising my estimate of them."

The waitress stepped over, and they both ordered the seafood platters with prawns, oysters, shrimp, and scallops. They then sat back. Stephanie buttered a roll and took a bite. Cat spread some artichoke dip on hers.

"So this psychiatrist thinks something is happening globally, something that might bring us closer together as a people?" Cat nodded her head. "Okay, I travel a lot and have seen some disturbing things. I mean, take India as an example. A guy gives me this wonderful book of ancient Hindu spirituality, but his country's city streets and the countryside roads are littered with the homeless and the hopeless."

"Yes. I can imagine. If you look around this restaurant, with all of these well-to-do diners, you can see the desperation lurking just below the surface."

"And this, whatever this is, can help remedy that?" Stephanie asked.

"We don't know. This outreach isn't some kind of humanitarian rescue mission, but more like an inner realignment, and not something we're controlling but only facilitating."

"I remember a line from that Hindu book, '*Brahman*, or their God, *is the creator*, not us.'"

Catherine nodded. Steph definitely got it. Their dinner was served, and they started eating and talking about their lives and what was happening around them. Stephanie moved in more elevated circles and shared insights and gossip about her world, its highs and lows. Catherine realized just how focused she had become on this new experience and dug deeper to share more personal tidbits about her life.

Finally, they finished dinner and their bottle of wine and sat back, drinking coffee before heading off into the night.

Then Stephanie broached the subject. "What does this have to do with us? I mean, why did you show up last night as you did and share this extraordinary dream experience?"

"As best as we can determine—that's Maria, her teacher Evelyn in England, and me—these dream states happen spontaneously and can't be directed, or at least the first connection to someone."

This clarification sounded promising to her. "You mean, now that we've connected, we can show up in the other's dream life?"

"Not quite, and it largely depends on one's intent, but the flow seems to be directed from something within our inner collective unconscious," Catherine said as her friend nodded tentatively. "Also, each time you 'share,' it shifts you and puts you in touch with some higher aspect of yourself. Why, last night, I told you sex would pull me away."

"And why do you think this inner something chose me if that's the case?"

"Let's face it, your social milieu is pretty dynamic, lots of movers and shakers."

Stephanie sat back. "I see, and you think I'll start having these waking dreams with my coterie of friends and expose them to this energy?"

"That's my best guess, but as I've experienced it, the impetus isn't coercive but participatory. You don't have to go along with it. I bet many don't."

"You know, last night at the fashion show and afterward at Saison, I could feel a shift, maybe seeing this scene with fresh eyes and realizing it's a dead end, at least for me. I've been to that mountaintop, and it holds no allure for me anymore."

The waitress stopped by and asked if they would like her to refresh their coffees. They declined, and Catherine took out her wallet. The waitress, Jill, a college student at UC Berkley, said the check was covered. She then thanked Stephanie for the generous tip. She had paid with her alias's credit card.

"So, if this happens with me, I'll go along with it. See where it leads me. But again, what about us?"

"You mean, in the romantic sense?"

"Yes, but after last night's dream time, sex seems less important. I mean, just getting off, if you'll excuse my language, pales in comparison."

"I've learned from my brief therapy that few things are either/or, and you just need to feel them out."

Stephanie smiled. "In that case, my agency has a room at the Ritz Carlton that I've booked for the night." Catherine nodded her head. "Now, I'm not suggesting we go there and get it on, but see where this leads us."

"Lead the way, my dear."

They both took their separate cars to the hotel, and the valets parked them. Catherine got the room number and suggested they take separate elevators or that she'd wait in the lobby for five minutes. They shouldn't go upstairs together. Stephanie agreed.

In the hotel room, she showed Catherine the array of nightwear in the clothes closet for them to wear. They both slipped into less provocative nightgowns and got into bed.

"How does this work? I mean, do we just fall asleep, or can I kiss you, or . . ."

"We like each other a lot. So we should physically express that, but what I sense is that if it gets too sexual, and not just kissing and caressing each other, it . . . dries up the dreaming energy."

"Okay."

Stephanie turned off the nightlamp on the side table. She turned and put her arms around Catherine and kissed her. Cat kissed her back, and Steph rolled over on top of her, and they made out for a while. Then, they both felt a shift of energy. Stephanie rolled off her lover, lay beside her as they quickly fell asleep, and had a most exquisite dream together, engulfed in this white light, and had never felt as loved. In the background, they could hear the giggles of little children.

11

London, England

Gerald Harris sat at his desk at MI5's offices in the Thames House, a historic building on the River Thames, which has served as the country's Internal Security headquarters since 1994. In recent weeks, he had been assigned to this peculiar waking dream phenomenon, given his background with Dr. Richardson and his history with her analysand Fyodor Makarov. They had found him and his family holed up in Edinburgh, Scotland with another Russian family. The cold weather and ocean breeze must've reminded him of his childhood in St. Peterburg, Harris figured. They offered him and his family police protection for cooperating with their investigation. They then relocated them to London. But, as Richardson and their experts had predicted, they couldn't control or target his so-called waking dreams or have him spy on people in the Kremlin. Since he had his last two episodes while off Clozapine, they stopped medicating him to provoke WDs, as they were now calling them. Unfortunately, this led to some schizoid incidents, and they put him back on the medication and looked for other subjects.

There was a knock on the door; then, someone pushed it open. It was Officer Davies. Harris waved him inside, and he stepped in and took a seat across from Harris. Davies then set his iPad on the desk and scanned through it.

"Whatchya got, Ron? Hope it's better than what I'm looking at. Probably more colorful." Like many of the old guard, Harris was resisting the move to the all-digital office. But at least he could print reports out and read the paper version.

"The BPS posting in its membership journal about waking dreams is getting a response." He looked down at the folder. "Some thousand psychiatrists worldwide have reported such patient episodes so far, along with shared dreams, which have a similar effect."

"More than I thought, but not over the top."

"That's if the doctors only had one dreaming patient each, so it could be double or triple that figure, and it's only been a couple of weeks. Yet the wide spread of the respondents makes it more of a global issue."

Harris nodded. "Anything noteworthy?"

"A lot of their patients have reported being seen and then seeing the other dreamer on another occasion."

"Let me get this straight. These patients have WDs of people, and later, the same person has waking dreams about them?"

"Also shared dreams. It's like a viral contagion," Davies said.

"And Patient Zero appears to be this Russian girl in Siberia?"

"Yes, but there's something else. Two of our subjects in America, this Dr. Amidala and her patient Ms. Dumont, along with Richardson, now have encrypted cell phones."

"Was that General Morton who clued us in about the Americans?"

"Yes, through our backchannel to him."

Harris sat back and gave this some thought. "Someone in this mix has viewed either our or the NSA's security meetings about phone and email intercepts and is alerting others?" Davies nodded his head. "Jesus, this sounds like the Cold War all over again."

"There is some good news. One of BPS's UK psychiatrists . . ." Davies looked down at his iPad and scanned through it, "is an asset, Dr. Cecil Graham. Maybe he'll cooperate with us since Richardson won't."

"Good. Bring him in and make sure he knows this inquiry falls under the National Security Act."

"Yeah, that oughtta loosen his tongue."

After Davies left, Harris scanned through his computer file on the DOD and retrieved Morton's number. He checked the time, called him in America, and was put on hold for five minutes before the general answered. He told him about their speculations.

"So Harris, what do we have here, a little psychic spy ring?" Morton asked.

"Wouldn't that be something? But I'm hoping it's less of a ring than this Russian girl tipping off your Dumont or Dr. Amidala."

There was a long pause. "The girl in contact with Major Bernard's son?"

"Yes." He paused. "Look, General. I'm bringing in an asset, a doctor treating one of these dreamers. I was thinking you could bring the Major's son in for a formal inquiry since, as you've reported, he's lying about further contact with the Russian girl."

Morton sighed. "I hate to go that far with kids."

"General, I've got a feeling, given that our Patient Zero is this little Russian girl, that this is spreading faster among children."

"Davies said the British journal people have gotten one thousand respondents." Harris didn't respond. "And since your security laws give you more leeway, why don't you see if that's the case? If so, I'll bring the boy in."

"Okay. But you might also talk with Dr. Amidala."

"That would be a bold move." He paused. "What? Try to turn her from adversary to asset. Yeah, I'll try that. Good thinking. And Harris, we need to keep this line open. This could be a major upheaval that won't be good for either of our countries. Shit, for the whole world."

The following day Davies brought in Dr. Graham. They met in the secure interrogation room. Again, some of the higher-ups were monitoring. Graham looked rather preppy in his pinstripe suit, with a pocket square of the same design and fabric. As advertised, he was a "with it" guy. After a few pleasantries, Harris got to the point.

"Dr. Graham, as my colleague Ron Davies has informed you, this investigation falls under the National Security Act. So despite your implied confidentiality with your patients, I need you to be forthright."

"I don't have a problem with that, sir. I signed on with you because the interests of our country supersede that of my analysands."

"Good. First of all. You reported that a patient of yours was having one of these waking dreams."

"Yes, a teenage girl with emotional issues saw a girl in Russia and had an exchange with her."

Harris looked at Davies. "A little blond-headed girl of ten or so?"

"No, a teenage girl of fifteen with striped hair, my patient's age."

"And did the girl come back and contact her at another time?" Harris asked.

"Yes." He paused. "So you're tracking this phenomenon?"

"Did the teenage girl say what city she was from?" Davies asked.

"No, but my patient saw a school banner and described it. I speak a little Russian, and it's in Kemerovo, Siberia."

Davies quickly looked it up on his laptop's browser. He turned to Harris. "It's 150 kilometers from Novosibirsk."

"Yes, that's the nearest big city in Siberia." The doctor paused for a long moment. "I don't know what your angle is here, but after several casual exchanges with this Russian girl, my patient's condition started to improve. It was as if she had integrated some of what was bothering her without much prodding by me."

Harris shook his head. "How's that, doctor?"

"She said it wasn't so much what the girl said, but the dreaming process connected her to . . . I know this will sound strange, but to God."

Harris looked totally baffled. Davies added, "Don't schizophrenics often have God delusions."

"Yes, but this girl isn't schizoid. She has or had a behavior disorder; now she's slowly becoming much calmer."

"How's that possible, doctor?" Davies asked.

Graham shook his head. "Never seen anything like it. Wish I could use these dream states as a therapeutic remedy."

Harris shook his head. "We'd rather you not encourage this . . . exploit, if we can call it that."

The doctor nodded. "Exploit? Very James Bond."

After the doctor left, they went back to Harris's office. He looked across the desk at his intelligence analyst. "Jesus, Davies. Is this girl recruiting others?"

Davies nodded. "That appears to be the case."

"And they might act as 'force multipliers?'"

"That would fit into the standard recruitment model." Ron thought for a moment. "But maybe they're not, if I may use the term, spreading this psychic contagion, but like with Graham's patient, they're looking for those to heal?"

"That's pretty much the whole damn human race."

"And that's bad?" Davies tentatively offered.

Harris looked askance at him. "Ron, if you haven't figured it out yet, we're in the 'separation' business. Keeping dangerous people isolated so they can't form groups and adverse political movements."

"I understand that. I majored in political science. But aren't healthy people more productive?"

"And more independent."

"I see," Davies said. "And the 'Internet of Things?'"

"Yes, but something we can control." He paused. "And ratchet up your monitoring of Richardson. Don't want her recruiting others."

This directive from his boss rubbed Davies the wrong way. On his way back to his office, Ron recalled a line from his favorite spy novelist John le Carré, "The secret services are the only real measure of a nation's political health. The one true expression of its subconscious." If that was indeed the case, this push to separate and isolate people instead of uniting them under a common cause like in Churchill's days didn't say much for the nation's subconscious health.

San Francisco, California

Alicia Holmes stepped into Dr. Amidala's office and was surprised to find another woman sitting with her. She had identified her agency and asked for a private meeting to discuss waking dreams and her experience with them. Maria pointed to the chair across from the colorful tartan sofa where they were sitting. All three women were wearing dark-colored pantsuits as if for psychic protection.

"I assume you're Catherine Dumont?" Alicia asked.

"In the flesh," she simpered.

"Which isn't always the case, is it?"

"It's Dr. Holmes, isn't it?" Maria asked, cutting off this line of inquiry. She nodded her head. "And your government agency is interested in waking dreams?" Another nod. "And why's that, Doctor?"

"Call me Alicia or Ms. Holmes. I'm a Ph.D., not a medical doctor like you." Alicia paused. "Okay. My SPS group at DARPA is investigating possible Black Swan developments."

"Unexpected but high-impact events," Maria replied. "And you think Catherine, who is no longer my analysand, I might add, and her waking dreams fit that criterion?"

"Dr. Amidala, we both know it's not just Ms. Dumont here having them. That it is, in fact, a global phenomenon, as your British Psychological Society has just uncovered."

"And what is it that you want from us?"

"Look, let's not dance around this inquiry. We know Dr. Richardson's patient, Fyodor Makarov, had an episode and viewed a meeting in the Kremlin. In addition, the Russian girl, Elena Mongush, who we're calling Patient Zero, has contacted people around the world. So the government is interested in where this might be heading."

"Because of its social impact?" Maria asked.

"Yes. A couple of thousand people communicating this way is one thing, but tens of millions, is quite another."

The two women across from her just glanced at each other but didn't reply. Alicia looked to Dr. Amidala. "Okay, we're just trying to ascertain the nature of this dreaming state. We have a report from a British psychiatrist that his teenage patient had several dream exchanges with someone and that it seemingly helped with her behavioral disorder."

Catherine added, "That's interesting, and what I'm experiencing myself." Maria looked at Cat and shook her head, but she continued, "They seem to help integrate issues of all kinds, and in some, it elevates their consciousness."

"Oh, my God," Alicia said.

Maria concurred. "Exactly, Ms. Holmes." She paused. "So your government group is probably wondering if people are using this access to spy on others when it's quite the opposite."

Alicia quickly recovered. "Or, that's one of its effects, but as Mr. Makarov has proven, not the only one."

Maria leaned over. "If I'm not mistaken, Makarov has a jaded history with his subject, and he was pretty locked into it. Maybe that prevented any change in behavior. Not what we've found in others."

"You're particularly well informed." She looked over at Dumont. "Or should I not be surprised?"

"Oh, so you think I'm spying on people?" Catherine asked.

Amidala added, "As you've mentioned, Dr. Richardson, my teacher and analyst, has shared her insights."

Alicia nodded her head. "Look, we're not adversaries, or don't have to be. We're just trying to understand the nature of this psychological state, if we can call it that." The two women nodded their heads. "I mean, why is it happening now?"

Maria looked to Catherine, then back at Dr. Holmes. "They seem spontaneous at first, and then people gravitate back to their contacts."

"Okay, but given its global nature, what or who's directing or facilitating these exchanges?"

Maria stared at the woman for a moment. "Your Ph.D. is in psychology?"

"Yes, I'm familiar with all the schools of thought and recently brushed up on Dr. Jung and his theories."

"Then, you won't be surprised by our theory that this is some aspect of our collective unconscious, maybe compensatory as we Jungians mostly characterize dreams."

Alicia sat back in her chair and sighed. "Thank you, Doctor. But I have to ask, compensatory to what? I understand Jung's dream concept, but what general attitude or orientation is it trying to balance off if I've got that right?"

"Maybe it's our global culture's shift from people's intuitive/feeling centers to our increasingly mental orientation."

"Okay, I get that," Alicia said. "But the big question is where is that leading us, and what will its impact be on our culture?"

"I can only answer that from my history with analysands needing to balance off their overly mental expression at the cost of their feeling nature."

"And, if I may ask, what effect does that have on their lives?"

Maria leaned forward again. "Depends on the severity of their mental fixation. Most experience a reordering of their values and priorities. Or, from the meaning of things to their value for them and others."

"And our global culture?"

"Less impactful in third world countries, I would think, highly impactful in the industrial countries with their overeducated populations. But given the increasing reliance on computers and the internet globally, that distinction may be outdated."

"A reordering of their values?"

"In India of the past, when Hindu men reached an advanced age, they reoriented their focus from the material world, or business pursuits, to the spiritual."

Alicia took a deep breath. "I see where this might be going, and if that happens in the general population, not just with the elderly, it could be cataclysmic for the Industrial West."

Catherine added, "It might, and it might not be. Many leaders in government and business blend the two. Take President Jimmy

Carter, a former military man, who's very religious and later focused on humanitarian endeavors."

"Yes, but the extreme Religious Right, claiming God's advocacy, has had its deleterious effect on politicians and our country's progressive swing for years."

"The difference is that people in touch with this energy have a much clearer contact with their, as some would call it, God-self, not their ego's fantasy spirituality."

"Let's hope so. I just fear the turmoil this might cause," Alicia said.

Maria nodded her head. "Yes, opening Pandora's Box releases good and evil influences, but that's the nature of evolutionary leaps."

This proposition didn't seem to mollify the security officer's concern.

Alicia finished their meeting and expressed her hope that whatever this was and wherever it was going, they could work together to mitigate any harmful effects. But there seemed to be little enthusiasm from them for any coordination. She had a plane to catch and hurried off. Her military attaché had a car waiting for her on the street. He whisked her off to the San Francisco Airport, where she took a United Airlines flight back to D.C. Emily had booked it and put her in First Class, given the possible fallout of her meeting here and the need for a bit of comfort.

It was late, and the plane was only half full. Alicia sat in the aisle seat, the window seat empty. She might need to rush to the bathroom, given her jittery stomach. While Amidala and Dumont were more cooperative than she had expected, the picture they painted wasn't reassuring, or at least not to her government sponsors. She had to laugh. "What if Elon Musk's focus on the heavens with his Space-X program was an early expression of this development, and it turned back on him? Jesus. This could get dicey."

Two hours into the flight, she felt some warmth to her right, as if someone's body heat. She turned and found Catherine Dumont's blurry image or spirit body, or whatever they called it, sitting next to her. A passing flight attendant didn't notice it.

She said, if not verbally, but what Alicia heard in her mind, "If you're willing, I can show you from personal experience its impact on people."

Alicia took a deep breath. She closed her eyes and could already feel a lightness of being even with this minimal contact.

"Okay. I'm open to it."

After a few moments, Alicia said, "Oh, my God."

A passing attendant asked, "Are you all right, ma'am?"

With her eyes still closed, she smiled and said, "Couldn't be better."

12

After work at the vast FSB building in Lubyanka Square, Galina Ilyin took the underground metro heading out of the downtown to the outskirts of Moscow and her apartment building. These central city stations, some of which were first designed in the 1930s, were architecturally stunning. They always reminded her of the old orthodox churches like St. Basil's that she had visited as a child. She would have preferred living within the Garden Ring that circled the city's hub if she could ever afford to live here. However, her aging father, Fedor, wanted to live outside the area, which reminded him of his old KGB haunts and life. As he once told her in an unguarded moment, "I have a lot to atone for. Don't need to be reminded of where all the bodies are buried."

The long ride often gave her a chance to review the day's work, and today had been particularly thorny. Given the expense of her Novosibirsk trip and its lack of results, her boss Yuri Belov had told her to drop this case. But she sensed that there was more to it. So today she stopped her research on paralytic neuromuscular blocking agents that could stop the heart from beating. Since they metabolize quickly, they could be used as a drug for foreign assassinations. Instead, Galina returned to the FSB online library and its

Google link and did another keyword search on waking dreams in Western magazines.

She did turn up a recent British Psychological Society inquiry to its members, asking if any psychiatrists had encountered this phenomenon. Galina did a browser search on the organization and discovered its vast worldwide membership. This inquiry was no small outreach and indicated that these so-called waking dreams could be more prevalent than she had imagined. Of course, there was the *Jung Journal's* inquiry from San Francisco, but what did you expect from California?

Without getting approval from Yuri, she filed an official request to have this British organization hacked to reveal these results. Admittedly, her justification was very speculative, but three children having these waking dreams in one classroom in Siberia, of all places, was statistically viable, or so she stated. Then, later that day, Yuri came over to her desk and was furious with her for filing this request without his approval. He told her to drop it in no uncertain terms or get formally reprimanded. Galina apologized; he had always been fair with her, and she knew this blunder also reflected on him and affected his career as well.

She got off at her station, dropped by the Perekrestok supermarket on her way home, and bought a roasted chicken; she didn't feel like cooking tonight. There was a light snow cover on the ground, but that didn't improve her dark mood.

At home, she slipped out of her military uniform and into sweatpants and a sweater. Her father was drinking a beer and watching a hockey game on TV in the living room. She looked over the kitchen counter and asked, "How about chicken tonight, Dad?"

He turned and looked over the sofa's back, his gray sweater worn thin at the elbows, his black-rimmed glasses with its right temple taped at the hinge. "If it isn't too much trouble, Galina," Fedor said tentatively. He hated imposing on his daughter, but his meager military pension left them no choice—a state institution or living with her.

"None. It's already cooked."

"Aw, such a modern girl," he laughed and returned to his game.

They engaged in light conversation at dinner, mostly about his day, since she couldn't share her top-secret work. Her father understood. But it became apparent to both of them that something was bothering her.

Finally, her father asked, "What gives, Galina? You're not your usual self tonight."

"Oh, Dad. It's nothing, just work stuff I can't talk about."

"Okay, but as we used to say back in my day, just talk around it."

Galina took a moment and carefully phrased her question. "Do you remember the government's psychic experiments in the 1970s and 80s?"

"Goes back further than that, but yes, we sometimes tried to use psychics to spy on Western consulates and agents."

"How did that go, Dad?"

"Very inconsistent, but enough to show it had promise." Her father paused for a moment. "But what captivated us at the KGB was a demonstration by one of these psychics using remote hypnosis. He went into a bank, just talked to a teller, and apparently hypnotized her to give him 100,000 rubles."

"I heard that story and thought it was folklore."

"No, I was one of the officers overseeing it. We then tried to use it to persuade a foreign agent to work for us, but it didn't work. The scientists said his counter-conditioning had blocked it. Of course, a little torture could overcome that, but not with foreigners." Her father stared at Galina. "Why is this coming up?"

"Dad. Really, I can't say."

"If it's in this area, don't discount whatever happens. I remember one of the scientists saying most coercive psychic tactics fail because they undermine what he called our moral conscience. Of course, we thought that was just bullshit back then, but I have to wonder about that now, given some of my regrets."

Galina took her father's hand. "Our good works redeem the bad we do."

"I think, to a point, but your generation's concept of bad doesn't, as they say, scratch the surface." Her father now stood up and started cleaning the table, his sign that this conversation was over. Afterward, they watched a BBC cop show, her father's favorite, before they both retired for the night.

The next morning, Galina thought her dream about little Elena Mongush was triggered by her father's dinner table conversation, but it felt so real. The girl was telling her to leave her and the other children alone. While her visage was the same sweet-smiling girl she had talked with at her school in Novosibirsk, Elena looked more resolved now. Of course, from psychology classes in college, she understood that the girl could represent another part of herself. But then, she recalled her father's talk with the Russian scientist and his concept of a moral conscience. Was that aspect of herself "talking to her?"

She just dismissed it and rode the metro to work that morning. When she got to her office, she could tell that Yuri was hyped up. He looked at her and just shook his head. When she turned on her computer, there was a message from the FSB Director to attend an 11 o'clock meeting in his office. She had never even met the man, but being called to his office couldn't be good.

"Yuri, you know what the Director's summons is about?"

"Guess it follows on yesterday's foreign hacking request, but I didn't imagine that would go this far up the line." He paused. "I don't know, Galina. But you might look around your desk and see what you want to box up and take home with you."

Galina shook her head. "Thanks, Yuri. Just what I need. A little moral support."

"You know how it is around here. Everybody's watching out for themselves."

Galina arrived for her meeting a half-hour early, as was the standard protocol to give the director some leeway with his always-busy schedule. Sometime later, a nonuniformed man in his forties with a short but stylish haircut stepped into the outer office carrying a briefcase. He gave the director's secretary a name and was ushered into his suite. A half-hour later, she called Galina to the office. The director, Grigori Tarasov, was seated at a work table with the other man. He was in his mid-fifties, still black-haired, with few wrinkles; unlike her father, he didn't appear to suffer from a bad conscience, or not yet.

Tarasov looked up. "Officer Ilyin, have a seat." She sat across from him, and he introduced the man, "This is SVR Deputy Director Ira Savin."

Galina was taken aback. There was a long-standing rivalry between their two agencies.

Sabin saw her reaction. "Yes, we've not always been on the best of terms with our sister agency, but this concern supersedes that contention."

"Yes, sir." Galina still looked puzzled.

Savin added, "My mother wanted a girl. At least she didn't call me Irina."

This remark got a laugh and broke the tension. Tarasov continued, "We are apprised of your research into this waking dream phenomenon and your interview with the children at the school in Novosibirsk. SVR has learned that this is a top priority of the British and American security agencies. Also, a Russian dissident in England apparently had one of these . . . episodes that revealed top-secret plans from behind Kremlin walls. So what can you tell us about this capability?"

Galina took a deep breath. "Director, our primary research subject is ten-year-old Elena Mongush at this school. She claims to have had two episodes, seeing her teacher's car getting back-ended and a schoolmate hit by a volleyball. They are both probably precognitive. But, as I said in my report, I believe she has had other episodes and that her teacher, Arina Dorzhiev, told her to keep quiet about them."

"She remote-viewed these incidents in some kind of dream state?"

"Yes, that appears to be the case."

Savin added, "The British are calling it that, or their cases, at least." He paused. "But nothing like what this . . ." He looked down at a folder, "Fyodor Makarov supposedly saw?"

"No, but again I've only interviewed this one girl and several of her classmates. However, I might note, as per my request yesterday, the British Psychological Society Journal put out a request to its 60,000 members about these waking dreams."

Director Tarasov leaned forward. "I had our people . . . look into that this morning, and it appears that they've had 1,000 respondents worldwide. Not a big number but, given this Kremlin episode, enough to warrant further investigation."

"Yes, sir."

"Is there any way of determining just how pervasive this phenomenon is in Russia?"

"Sir, we could follow the British lead and have the RPS, the Russian Psychological Society, send out a similar inquiry." The Director nodded his approval.

Savin added, "And since MI6 calls this Mongush girl Patient Zero, contact the Pediatricians of Russia organization and have them make a similar inquiry."

Galina looked to Director Tarasov. "Good idea. And let's bring this little girl back here and explore the nature of this phenomenon." He paused. "I'm putting you in charge of a joint task force with the SVR to explore this development."

Galina nodded her head but looked a bit shaken. "Is there something wrong, Office Ilyin?"

"Sir, last night I had a dream in which Elena came to me and told me to 'leave her and the other children alone.'"

Savin said, "Ha. All the more reason to proceed since there are other children involved."

Director Tarasov agreed. "Have our resident agent in Novosibirsk round her up and fly her back here."

Galina nodded her head. "I have been in contact with Officer Stepanov there."

"Good. I've allocated offices for you down the hall from STS, with a secretary to coordinate. I want you to survey our Emergent Science applicants and pick a recruit to help you with your investigation." He now turned to Savin. "The Deputy Director will assign an SVR officer at their end to coordinate with you."

"Yes, sir. And I take it that this is Top Secret and on a need-to-know basis?"

"You've got that right." There was a long pause. Galina looked hesitant. "Is there anything else, Officer?"

"Just how critical is this . . . inquiry, sir?"

Tarasov looked over at Savin and then back at Ilyin. "Officer, as you know, we maintain an orderly society in Russia by clamping down on dissent elements, here and abroad. We have many tools at our disposal for that, some of which were developed by your scientific division. But this psychic virus is mostly, if I understand it, untraceable. And I'm not just talking about secret communication or even psychic spying, but what if this develops into a religious or spiritual experience? As Lenin said in another era, which still holds true, 'Religion is the opium of the people.' So, Officer, treat this as religious counterterrorism, as our Chinese friends do."

Galina stood up. "Yes, sir."

"You're dismissed, Officer. And good work."

When Galina returned to her science office, she started to box her belongings. Yuri assumed the worst. "Sorry, Galina. Was it that bad?"

"No, actually, I'm moving down the hall to new offices as head of a joint task force."

"No kidding? On these waking dreams?"

"Can't say more, but you can piece it together from yesterday's inquiry."

Yuri nodded. "Just remember your friends as you move up the line."

"And not just look out for me like everybody else?"

Yuri squinched his mouth and said, "*Ox*" (Yikes).

Once she got situated in her new office, and after technical services hooked up her computer and phone, Galina called Officer Stepanov.

"You're kidding, Ilyin."

"No, not at all. Pick up the Mongush girl at school and take her home to pack a bag. Tell her parents we need to talk with her in Moscow about her daydreams. But we'll take good care of her."

"And if they resist?"

"Call in the local police, but I want both of you on a flight this evening. Call me with the airline's arrival time."

"I don't like this at all, Officer?"

"Would you like me to have Director Tarasov confirm it?"

"*Robho* (shit). Okay, I'll get back to you shortly. Email me the paperwork."

"And Stepanov, don't tell anybody about this, not your regional supervisor, nobody. If they have a problem with that, have them call the Director's office."

Later that afternoon, Office Stepanov called in the flight's arrival time and that he had picked up the girl. Galina had an official car drive her to Sheremetyevo International Airport to meet their flight that night, but Stepanov and the girl were not on the plane. Calls to him and the girl's parents went unanswered.

13

London, England

Evelyn and Maria Amidala hurried into Richardson's apartment, set their blue Jung Symposium folders on the dining room table, and headed for the kitchen. They poured themselves shots of Glenfiddich scotch and drank them straight down.

"Let's not make a habit of this," Evelyn said. "But can you believe that opening session? I mean, I had just suggested to Sarah Townes that she include waking dreams in her keynote speech but never realized what an uproar that would cause."

"As we Americans would say, 'The shit has hit the fan,'" Maria added.

They now stepped into the small living room and sat in padded chairs across from each other. They both closed their eyes to center themselves. It had all been a bit unsettling. As soon as Dr. Townes mentioned the topic of "waking dreams," hands shot up. The usually sedate and polite psychiatrists started spontaneously airing their concerns about this dream state and its effect on their analysands. As best as they could determine, listening to these doctors and looking at the faces of the more reticent but still concerned participants, many of them were now dealing with this phenomenon. Responses from Maria's early journal request had seemingly just skimmed the surface. Finally, Evelyn walked up to the stage to intervene. She told the audience that she and Dr. Amidala from San Francisco had been investigating these waking dreams and would hold a forum tomorrow to address everybody's concerns. That had at least quieted the storm.

The next afternoon their Special Session was moved to the main hall, given the number of attendees. As a leading member of the Society, Evelyn gave an overview of waking dreams from a Jungian perspective, excluding its political fallout. They then called for questions. The first centered around psychiatrists whose analysands were experiencing spontaneous improvement of various disorders after several dream episodes.

A psychiatrist from France, Felix Boucher, said, "As Jungians, we all know the power of archetypes to heal various symptoms by revealing hidden unconscious aspects of a person that need integration. We usually deal with that in dreams, but these waking dreams don't seem to be therapeutic in that regard. Yet, two of my analysands, whose encounters or visions of other people's lives, which aren't compensatory or symbolic in any meaningful way, experienced some psychological relief. It was as if they were infused with mana or light. Their fixation or repression just started to integrate a bit. Of course, more work needs to be done, but I'm puzzled."

Evelyn explained, "That is definitely happening within their personal unconscious, but it seems to be directed by the Collective Unconscious. So, like denied aspects of an individual, they may also represent denied collective aspects of humanity. It's like what happens with personal dream symbology, how awareness leads to an integration of psychic energy. This process of sympathetically seeing and connecting to others, all discrete parts of humanity as a whole, is like a collective dream and works to heal both the individual and the collective, or so I would imagine."

Another psychiatrist, Dr. Eric Jordan from Lancashire, raised his hand and was called. "I mainly deal with children in my practice, and I must say that every one of them is experiencing these episodes. Of course, you can't analyze children like adults and delve into their dream symbology as thoroughly, but they seem to get progressively more integrated as the waking dreams happen. And Dr. Boucher's mana reference seems applicable here. It's like they're infused with light. I can't explain that. Can either of you?"

Evelyn added, "Again, it seems to be the process of the dream connecting them to the archetype of the Self, the healing center of our lives, individually and collectively, as you well know. And young children are closer to it than us adults and might call it God."

A black-clothed Jesuit doctor, Mateo Russo, added, "If I may quote Dr. Jung, 'I have had the experience of being gripped by something that is stronger than myself, something that people call God.'"

Another participant added, "Amen, Father."

The priest added rather sheepishly, "And Christ did heal people instantaneously."

A few of the psychiatrists rolled their eyes. Evelyn looked to Dr. Amidala to change the subject. Maria asked, "Dr. Jordan, if I may ask, are any of your children interacting with a blond ten-year-old Russian girl?

This question startled him. "Yes, they are, or a few of them at least. Does that have any significance?"

At that moment, Richardson looked out into the audience and spotted Officer Davies from MI5 sitting in the back row and taking notes on an iPad. She stepped over and whispered in Maria's ear. Catherine then told the doctor to meet her later for a more thorough exchange. The others found this curious, but other questions quickly arose about this waking dream state, and the session continued.

The focus had seemingly shifted to the Jungian concept of the Self. For Carl Jung, the Self is the archetype of wholeness, the unified personal consciousness—the ego—and the unconscious. This archetype is about the individuation of a person, which is the goal of therapy. Von Franz called the Self, "A sort of hidden regulating or directing tendency . . . [an] organizing center in the personality." This tendency was further elucidated by Jung later in his career as the *Objective Psyche*. This function is a self-conscious force that, through dreams and intuitions, nurtures the development of the individual in their quest for self-actualization. But, despite Richardson's clarification, some psychiatrists were still struggling with this concept.

Finally, a London-based psychiatrist, Dr. Earl Livingston, put this speculation into a stark perspective. "So you're saying the Collective Unconscious, which represents a Collective Self, or a self-organizing center for all humanity, is orchestrating some kind of therapy ending in humanity's eventual individuation as a species at some future point?"

The mere idea seemed to shock those present resulting in a few gasps and uneasy body shudders. "Please, somebody, tell me I'm overstating it?" the doctor pleaded.

Then, suddenly, Livingston closed his eyes. "Wait, I seem to be having one of these waking dreams." Others in the audience, not everyone, closed their eyes simultaneously.

Dr. Richardson quickly responded, "Earl, describe what you're seeing?"

"A young woman, American by her dress, twentysomething, blond hair, is standing in a field. Now pinpoints of light, not particles but maybe tiny shining faces, are appearing in her, one by one, then more and more." Some doctors in the audience nodded their heads. *"They're accelerating,*

and now her whole body is blazing with this light, the aforementioned mana, I assume. Still, I have the sense she's not overwhelmed by it, that she's part of it, and it's part of her."

Livingston opened his eyes and sat back in his chair but seemed overwhelmed by this vision.

Evelyn said, after coming round, "I think that woman demonstrated how the personal consciousness can merge into the collective and still be its own discrete self."

Maria added, "Or how we are all part of a single group soul."

Livingston jumped up from his seat and shook himself as if sloughing off something. "I don't know about the rest of you, and excuse my indelicacy, but I need a drink."

"And with that, this Special Session is closed," Richardson announced.

Some doctors stood up and rushed out, while others remained in their seats, settling the experience. When they opened their eyes, they seemed charged with a new resolve.

Evelyn and Maria waited for the hall to clear, and then Richardson spotted Officer Davies in the back row, his eyes still closed. They walked down the aisle to where he was sitting and stood there until he opened his eyes.

"Are you all right, Davies?" Evelyn asked.

He nodded his head and came around, taking a deep breath. "Yes, but that was quite an experience. Was the woman Catherine Dumont?"

Maria was reluctant to share that information, but Evelyn sensed that Davies had been greatly affected by this dream state, and she would tell him. "Yes."

He nodded and said, "Oh, incidentally, MI6 'heard' that the little Russian girl, Elena Mongush, has disappeared."

Novosibirsk, Russia

Officer Kostya Stepanov arrived at Elena Mongush's primary school at 2:00 pm. He now carried a formal FSB detention notice, but he still encountered heavy resistance to his orders from her teacher Arina Dorzhiev and the school principal, Dima Kozlov. Elena just smiled at them and agreed to go with the police officer. At her home, the girl's parents couldn't understand what the country's internal security wanted with a ten-year-old. It wasn't like she was a terrorist or had caused any trouble for the government.

Stepanov explained, "You know about her waking dreams?"

Both parents begrudgingly nodded, but her father, Vadim, said, "So she daydreams about other people. How is that a security issue?"

"Mr. Mongush, I wish I knew. I was just given the order to transport her to Moscow by FSB Officer Galina Ilyin. She interviewed Elena at her school and is now heading up a task force about these dreams. Galina will take good care of your daughter."

Her mother helped Elena pack a small suitcase with enough clothes to last a week. The girl insisted on taking her heavy winter clothes, although it wasn't as cold in Moscow as here this time of year. The two of them left at 4:00 pm for their 7:00 pm flight. Since Elena hadn't had dinner yet, Officer Stepanov found a roadside diner near the airport for them to eat. The meals on Russian airlines were notoriously bad. After they sat down and ordered, Kostya had a moment to check his unfamiliar feelings of grave concern about this detention order. What was happening here? What would they do to this sweet little girl in Moscow? He had heard stories from his father about ESP experiments on children back in the old days at Akademgorodok.

Sitting across from Elena at the diner, Kostya had what he assumed was one of these waking dreams. *It showed the girl in an interrogation room at FSB headquarters subjected to intense questioning. She was crying and protesting that she didn't contact people in America or anywhere else. Finally, an officer slapped the girl's face and told her to stop lying.*

He came back or woke up from this daydream and looked over at Elena. He now felt even more concerned about this young girl, like it was his responsibility to save her from such mistreatment. But was he willing to jeopardize his career and his family's safety?

"Elena, I'm not sure about taking you to Moscow."

"I don't want to go there, Officer. We could stay with my friend Inna in Kemerovo in the mountains. I've already talked with her, and her family will let us stay there."

Elena reached her hand across the table and took Kostya's. "The soldier woman who came to see me. She's on our side; she just doesn't know it yet." Kostya closed his eyes as a wave of energy surged through him.

"Excuse me, but I have to go to the bathroom." There he splashed water on his face. Was he out of his mind? Was this little girl psychically manipulating him? Then, suddenly, he saw a picture of a woman in the bathroom mirror. She looked American.

"You'll be okay, Kostya. There's more at stake here than you can imagine," she said in Russian, *if with an accent.*

"Who are you, and how are you doing this?" he asked sharply.

"Elena is part of a movement to help heal people across the globe. Eventually, you will be considered a hero for saving this little girl."

"Or, put to death as an American spy."

"The powerful will soon be powerless; mark my word."

He rushed to the toilet and threw up his meal. He felt better afterward. Kostya sat on the toilet seat and could feel his emotions settling, and a new resolve overtook him. He had not always been motivated to do what was right, except for his family. Maybe his definition of family was expanding. Back at the table, Kostya took out his cell phone to chart a route to Kemerovo.

Elena reached out and stopped him. "You have to throw your phone away. They can track us with it."

Stepanov shook his head. "For an innocent little girl, Elena. You know a lot about how the world works."

"It's easy when you can move through the world's psychic currents. I will teach you."

"I must be out of my mind, but let's go. I'll stop off and get a map at a service station."

"You don't need a map. I know the way," Elena said.

Kostya dropped his cell phone in the trash on the way out. A teenage boy spotted it and reclaimed it after they left. He switched the sim card at home, erasing all the man's contacts and phone logs.

That night after they got settled at Inna's house in Kemerovo, Elena had a waking dream with her teacher, Arina Dorzhiev. She was sitting in bed reading before going to sleep. Elena appeared in her dreaming body.

"Ms. Dorzhiev, I just wanted to tell you I'm all right."

"Elena, how are you doing this?"

"It's like with my visions. The American woman calls it a waking dream."

"Wow, that's amazing."

"Would you like to join us? Help us spread the energy?"

Arina closed her eyes and could feel this incredible flow of energy directed at her.

"Yes. I would. Very much."

Elena stepped forward and took Arina's hands, and the woman became infused with light.

Afterward, she asked, "How do I share this with others?"

"It will come to you, and just follow the energy trail."

After a few waking dreams that week, Arina appeared to her father in the dream state and shared this light energy with him. After that, he no longer jumped at the door knocks.

14

London, England

Ron Davies lived in an old 19th-century building in Fitzrovia, within walking distance of the University of London. It was a central district with museums and galleries, bistros and cafes. Today, after this rather remarkable Jung Symposium session, he headed to a nearby café for a couple cups of espresso, not liquor, as Dr. Livingston had facetiously suggested. Before he fell down Alice's rabbit hole, he needed to break the hold this waking dream had on him, even if he liked this euphoric feeling. He didn't want to numb himself, just wake up. Ron sat at a corner booth, and one expresso did bring him back. He ordered a shepherd's pie for dinner, hoping this old family dish would further ground him.

He closed his eyes, but this light-filled image of Catherine Dumont still lingered. With her palms out, the woman had reminded him of something when she first appeared, and now he could relate it to iconic childhood images of the Virgin Mary. Unlike his mostly protestant colleagues at work, Ron had been raised Catholic, even if he stopped practicing as a rebellious teenager. But, as the child psychiatrist at the symposium, Dr. Jordan would undoubtedly agree our childhood experiences, good or bad, always remain with us. Finally, the shepherd's pie arrived, and he tore into it like it was mana from the heavens. The food warmed him up on this cold, dreary day.

Afterward, he sat back and wondered if it was the purity of this image and its holy reference that moved him so much. In his early thirties, he was still a bachelor and enjoyed a fairly active sex life with various women. He felt no guilt about it, although his two married brothers would constantly prod him at family get-togethers about settling down. At least their offspring gave his parents the requisite grandchildren they wanted, and they didn't hound him for more. Then, one of his casual hookups stepped into the café with a girlfriend and waved at him. Ron shook his head. He wanted to be alone tonight. Calling his waitress over, he paid the bill and left before the fiery redheaded Emily forced herself on him, with her big tits pressed against his arm and driving him to distraction.

At home he placed his iPad on his office desk. He went into the living room and sat on the sofa. Ron looked at his wide-screen TV and thought about checking out a hockey game or a film on one of the movie channels. But he wasn't in the mood for anything distracting. So he just sat there as the sunlight seeped out of the day, and his apartment grew dark. Years ago, Ron had been in therapy and knew to feel his way through what was bothering him. He realized that besides the Jung's group waking dream and its bright, soothing light, Dr. Livingston's clarification of where this movement may lead them had intrigued him. Was there something in the collective unconscious really pushing the human race toward some spiritual apotheosis? He could just see Harris's jaundiced reaction tomorrow to his symposium notes on this speculation.

He remembered a Jesuit priest telling his religion class in high school that it was our spiritual obligation to uplift humanity. We shouldn't further degrade it by loose behavior or attack its religious foundation, no matter the faith. He thought he had left all that hokum behind with his university education. But he had to admit that something was missing in his life, not a wife, children, or career advancement. As Jung or von Franz might say from Ron's study of their work, there was "a hole in his staircase"—a transitional stage missing or undeveloped. Maybe for him and humanity as a whole. This new focus at his security agency on learning about and possibly suppressing people's waking dream experiences and where it might lead them, definitely outside of governmental control, as Harris had suggested, was now a concern.

Tired and a bit overwhelmed, Ron lay his head down on the sofa in the dark and quickly fell asleep. *He dreamed of himself as a little boy again, and a blond-headed girl was holding his hand and pulling him through a field of daisies. It felt so fresh and invigorating. Was this the field near his home growing up in the country? She spoke to him with an accent and told him that he should serve life, not suppress its unfolding.* He woke up somewhat startled but feeling relieved and maybe charged up. The little girl looked very familiar. Ron flipped on the overhead light and went into his office. He turned on his iPad and typed the security codes to reach the MI5 mainframe. He called up the photo of Elena Mongush, who had been appearing to people worldwide and who had recently disappeared. It was the girl from his dream. Apparently, she had reached out to him. He definitely wouldn't share that with Harris.

AT WORK LATE the following morning, Gerald Harris called Ron into his office. His boss had printed out his notes from yesterday's Jung Symposium and laid them on his desk. He looked at Ron and didn't seem very pleased.

"Tell me about this, Dr. Livingston fellow. Is the guy just a crackpot suggesting that these little daydream episodes are leading us to Armageddon?"

"Sir, I wouldn't characterize it as that dire. I mean, the human race could use an upgrade."

Harris shook his head. "Keep on point, Davies."

"I've delved into his background this morning, thinking a lot hinges on his analysis." Ron looked down at his iPad. "He's well respected with several solid books on Jung and his theories, and his extension of them." He paused. "But to be fair to the good doctor, yesterday he was just summating where these inquiries from the other doctors were leading everybody."

"Oh, that's a relief, Davies. So it's not just him spouting off, but all of these well-respected crackpots."

"They're not crackpots, sir; they are just as concerned as we are about this phenomenon."

Harris shook his head dismissively. "You don't say. Come on, Ron. Get with the program. Give me something I can hang my hat on."

"Well, it is accelerating globally, and I don't know how we can intervene. We can't tell people to stop having them since it seems beyond their control."

Harris sat back and thought this through. "But is it 'beyond their control?'" Harris opened his file drawer, searched it, and pulled out a large file. He turned to the back and read a report.

Davies could guess at his approach. "You're thinking about the Russian dissident, Fyodor Makarov, and that he was off his antipsychotic medication when he had his two episodes."

Harris looked across at his assistant. "Jesus, Davies. Did that group daydream yesterday leave you psychic or something?"

"No, just following the logic trail, sir." He paused. "But we can't douse the English water supply with clozapine and hope for the best."

Harris sniggered. "Wouldn't that be something? No, we substitute self-control for drugs and get the same effect. We have our own authorities and our allies issue warnings that individuals need to suppress these waking dreams. I never dream because I don't want to hear about it. If not, they could lead to serious psychological problems and even mass psychosis, like what overtook Germany in the 1920s. That might shut it down."

"While our enemies in Russia and China figure out a way to use them to their advantage?"

"Is that possible, Ron?"

"I don't know, sir. But before we jump the gun, as they say, we need to consider this solution more carefully. I mean, without proper preparation, this could create mass panic."

"Maybe we don't have a choice. Give me some options, Ron. Draw on any resources you need but do it quickly. I'm getting pressed from above."

Davies stood up. "Okay." He turned and walked away and couldn't help but smile to himself. After he left, Harris thought about it, picked up the phone, and called the head of MI5.

Fort Collins, Colorado

Catherine flew into the Denver airport and rented a car to make the 70-mile drive to Fort Collins. She could've taken a commuter flight from here to a regional airport twenty miles south of the city, but she wanted to take this long drive through familiar territory. She loved seeing the snow on the ground. Didn't get that in San Francisco. It was early December, and Cat would miss the two big end-of-the-year holiday celebrations by design, much to her mother's dismay. But they were both shocked and delighted that she was visiting them. She hadn't been home in two years, but this was far from a family visit. Given what was transpiring with her and others across the globe, she wanted to talk with her father, whose metaphysical background might give her a broader perspective or further nauseate her.

She realized too late as she pulled into their crowded circular driveway that she should have timed her arrival for earlier in the day and not shown up at dinnertime. Instead, Catherine walked into a festive gathering of relatives and friends. Some of them were dressed in last year's Christmas sweaters. She sat on the oversized living room couch, sipping the spiked eggnog and answering questions about her life in San Francisco.

In his red reindeer sweater, her Uncle Henry, the inappropriate one, finally asked, "Is the city as gay as they say? I mean, I've seen their Gay Parade on TV." He paused, getting a jaundiced look from his wife. "It was pretty . . . colorful."

"Did you spot me in the middle holding hands with some of my gay girlfriends?" Cat teased but caused more than a few gasps.

In her customary blue moose sweater, her mother, Joyce, narrowed her eyes, then added, "You know, Cat. She's such a kidder." Then she caught herself, just in case. "Not as if that would be wrong." The others reluctantly nodded their heads.

Her mother had cooked another huge turkey with all the fixings for the gathering. As the family sat down at the long mahogany table and surveyed this feast, another uncle said, "Perfect timing, Cat. We get two of Joyce's fabulous Thanksgiving dinners this year."

"No doggy bags, James," Joyce said.

His wife Marty added, "As if any dog could love him." Ouch.

It didn't take long for the normalcy of it all to seep into Catherine's bones. The last four months, and more recently with the accelerating waking dream syndrome, as Maria was now calling it, had been bizarre and a little unnerving. Finally, Catherine joined in the spirit of the reunion and answered her family's inquiries about work, life in the Bay Area, and her friends. She mentioned that her best friend was the model Stephanie Taylor, for which there was a lot of interest, male and female. She explained that she rented a loft from her boyfriend in Mill Valley, and that's how they met. To her surprise, Catherine found that she liked connecting with family and friends again. Maybe she needed to come back more often to her "human roots," as Evelyn called it.

She looked over at her mother and father and could sense or feel how she had ostracized herself from them and now felt terrible about that. Teenagers and young adults try to establish their independent selves and lives, and in her case, to extricate herself from their New Age craziness, which wasn't so crazy after all. But she never doubted their love for her. She now had to admit that love wasn't reciprocated as well as it could have been while growing up. As they looked back at her beaming their love and approval, Cat was able to send them from the depths of her being her, until now, unexpressed love and appreciation of who they were as two souls searching for a way back to their Source, as we all are.

Finally, after three hours, Joyce shooed everybody away. Cat tried to help her mother clean the table, but she wouldn't hear of it. "I assume this isn't just a family visit but something you and your father need to talk about."

"Ah, I forgot how psychic you are, Mom," Catherine said.

She smiled. "Mothers are naturally tuned into their daughters, psychic or not."

Her father rekindled the logs in the fireplace, and soon they had a warm and blazing fire again. Catherine sat on the couch while Barry pulled a chair across from her.

"So, kiddo, what's on your mind?"

As was customary with her, Catherine got to the point and told him about her waking dream experience and what was happening to others worldwide. However, she didn't want to send him off on a tangent, so she left out the more far-ranging speculation or the white-light experience some of them were having.

"Dad, given your metaphysical background, I figured you might have a thought or two about it."

"You bet," he chuckled. "The end result, if not this dreaming process itself, but still a possible route, sounds like what Sri Aurobindo and Pierre de Chardin saw as the goal of human evolution."

"I remember you mentioning de Chardin," she said. "And the other pundit is some Indian guru?"

"Aurobindo, drawing on the ancient *Upanishads*, tells how the divine spark was innate in matter and evolved matter into life and life into mind ending with the evolution of what he called the Supermind, or a collective whole."

"Isn't that what de Chardin was getting at?"

"Yes, but he didn't know of Aurobindo's work until later in his life but saw that their conclusions were basically the same. While the Indian presented this speculation using Hindu thought, de Chardin came to his overview from a Western philosophical perspective."

"Really, I took philosophy courses in college and didn't come across this kind of speculation."

"De Chardin shows in his books how this concept was embedded in Western thought going back to Heraclitus, Plato, Plotinus, and more recently, in Nietzsche and Bergson."

"I guess that's reassuring, but the whole movement toward that point will cause a lot of personal and global upheavals. I can't help but recall Dr. Amidala's quoting the Bible, 'It's a fearful thing to fall into the hands of the living God.'"

"Amen, sister," Barry said. He looked at his daughter. "And you can share this experience with others?"

"Yes, and most people don't have the same overreaction I had at first."

"Remember the 100th Monkey Effect? How after lots of people learn a new idea or have a new experience; it's easier for others to absorb it."

"Yeah, I vaguely remember you going on about that."

Barry stepped over to the couch, sat next to his daughter, and stuck out his hand. Catherine took it, and her father closed his eyes. He wouldn't need much of a charge.

Joyce watched this exchange from the hallway and stepped over.

"Hey, don't leave me out."

She now sat down on the other side of her daughter. Joyce smiled and took her hand, and Cat infused them with this light energy. The Christian directive, "Where three or more gather in my name," seemed to be the magical formula that created an energy bubble spreading out from their house into the neighborhood. Three blocks away, Uncle Henry woke up and just absorbed the light energy. "Thanks, Cat," he said and lay his head back on the pillow as he reached over and touched his sleeping wife.

15

Falls Church, Virginia

Alicia called Greg to pick her up at Reagan National Airport on her flight from San Francisco. She was still overwhelmed from her waking dream with Catherine Dumont on the flight. She wasn't dreamy or out of it, just inwardly focused and strangely energized. Alicia looked at her hands to ensure that light wasn't pouring out her fingers. She remembered her yoga teacher talking about raising one's kundalini energy up the spine and imagined it felt like that. Luckily, Alicia had taken a cab to the airport from their DARPA office in Arlington because she couldn't drive home now and deal with all the hustle and bustle of freeway traffic. She was in a relationship with Greg, but they were careful not to disclose it to anybody at the office. Since SPS was independent of that agency and fraternization rules were not set up for their group, they felt free to get involved but kept it quiet.

Her trip today was a back-and-forth excursion, and she didn't take luggage, just a laptop and a purse, which she flopped on the backseat of Greg's black BMW Sports Coup as he pulled up to the curb. Alicia had been vague on the phone about why she didn't take a cab, but he knew there was more to it and didn't mind picking her up. This way, she'd sleep over with him and not go directly back to her apartment in Annandale. He drove off and looked over at her, but Alicia was somewhat distant.

Finally, Greg asked, "How did it go?"

She turned to him, still very pensive. "The meeting went fine, and I have some updates."

Alicia turned back and looked out the window. The lights of the suburban malls and housing tracts helped bring her back.

Greg drove on, but her mood or deep introspection alarmed him at some point. It wasn't like her. "Is everything all right, Alicia?" No response. "You seem a bit . . . out of it."

She turned back to him. "I had one of those waking dreams on the flight back, or Catherine Dumont appeared in the ethers and offered to show me their impact on people. And if this is the general effect, it will wake people up."

Alicia saw that Greg was about to take the Falls Church exit from the freeway. "Greg, I'm not sure I'll be great company tonight. Maybe you should drop me off at my place."

"So you can go further astray or to wherever this took you. No. Come back with me, and let's talk, just talk."

She placed a hand on his arm. "Thanks. You're probably right."

Alicia took a shower at his apartment and changed into casual night clothes she kept there. When she walked into the kitchen, Greg had already boiled water, made instant coffee, and micro-waved some chicken quesadillas.

"That's great. I'm starving. Couldn't eat on the plane. Pretty out of sorts when I . . . came back."

Greg held off the questions and let Alicia drink some coffee and wolf down the Mexican food. Finally, he asked, "Let's talk about the meeting first. Maybe as far as we go tonight."

"Yes, Dr. Phil," she teased. "No, really, that would be better." They moved into the living room and sat on the sofa. Alicia gave him a brief rundown of her meeting with Dr. Amidala and Catherine Dumont and its far-ranging speculation.

Finally, Greg sighed. "Wow. So humanity could be the patient, and these dreams might compensate for our overly mental orientation as a species, or what's keeping us apart? A classic counterpoint between the mind and heart."

"Yes, but her example of people, like elderly Hindu men switching from a material-world focus to a spiritual one, could get a bit dicey if applied to all of us. I can just see Morton decrying that."

"At least," Greg said with a laugh.

Alicia closed her eyes. "Wait a minute. It's coming back to me." She paused for a long moment. "It felt like she took me through a collective unconscious stream to a source point of some nature full of this amazing light, the Self, as Amidala said, where we are all of one mind. It felt extraordinary. I could see people of all nationalities flowing through it, fed by this light and replenishing themselves. I didn't want to leave, but Catherine pulled me back."

She opened her eyes and took a long sip of her coffee. "It changed everything for me. If this is where this experience is all leading us, I can't suppress it. May even be some kind of evolutionary leap like you suggested to Blackman."

Greg looked back at her. "Let's not get ahead of ourselves. For now, don't share your waking dream or these insights with anybody else at the office."

"I'll just keep to the script and only talk about my conversation with Amidala and Dumont." She paused. "But you and I won't drop this inquiry, right?"

"No, my dear. There's more at stake here than people spying on others." Alicia looked around his living room. Greg smiled. "I sweep for bugs once a year."

Alicia yawned and stood up. "Let's hit the sack. The next couple of weeks should be interesting."

GENERAL MORTON, who had been out of the country for a week, called for a group meeting the following Monday. After everyone had gathered, he first asked Alicia about a rundown of last week's meeting with Dr. Amidala in San Francisco. When she mentioned that Catherine Dumont came to it, Morton nodded as if he expected that.

After she finished, Greg added, "It seems they're saying that humanity is the patient, and these waking dreams might compensate for our overly mental orientation to bring society, as it would an individual, into a more balanced whole?"

General Morton sighed. "Greg, you're ahead of the curve like always." He pulled out a sheet of paper from his valise. "There was a Jung Symposium in London this past week. Maria Amidala was in attendance. She must've flown out shortly after she met with Alicia. I flew into London on my trip back from a NATO conference in Brussels and dropped in on MI5. One of their men monitored the Symposium. Here's what a Dr. Livingston said along the same lines as Greg."

Morton put on his wire-rimmed reading glasses. "So you're saying the Collective Unconscious, which represents a Collective Self, or a self-organizing center for all humanity, is orchestrating some kind of therapy ending in humanity's eventual individuation as a species at some future point?"

He now looked around the table. "Their eggheads filled me on the Jungian jargon." He looked over at Greg and Alicia sitting next to each other. "You're the psychologists, and we are all the forecasters. So what does this Black Swan development mean for the security of our nation and its people?"

Greg said, "General, if these waking dreams and their effect on people continue unabated, a lot of personal, and I might add, national boundaries will crumble."

"Shit. I was afraid of that." He now looked around the table. "What are we going to do about that?"

Everyone looked at each other, wondering if they should do something about its spread. But none of them offered any off-handed suggestions. Finally, Eric Darby added, "Maybe it's time we talked with the DARPA geeks about a technofix. I mean, dreams are formulated in discrete areas of the brain, and it's been shown that certain sound frequencies can dampen some brain centers."

Greg was quick to add, "Whoa. Whether we remember them or not, dreams are essential for mental health. Dream deprivation, especially the lack of REM sleep, can cause severe mental problems. We must consider whether there's any correlation between these waking and sleeping dreams. We can't just send sound waves through TV and radio transmissions and dampen them."

Morton considered this reservation. "I understand we don't want to go from bad to worse, but we can at least bring the geeks into this case and see what they say."

Greg looked at Alicia. They both had the same thought. The situation had already gone from bad to worse.

San Francisco, California

Maria sat on her deep-stained wooden patio, sipping a glass of Chianti and watching the sunset on the horizon. There was no chance of catching the green flash again with thin white clouds on the horizon today. That was almost a relief. The past couple of weeks were filled with unconscious feedback, personal and collective, and she didn't need a further reminder of it from the denizens down under, as it were. The Jung Symposium had been historic, as one psychiatrist labeled it. She had missed the final day. At Evelyn's suggestion, Maria had changed her flight and slipped out of England before British Security could draw her in for a debriefing. As it turned out, her teacher was right. They came to the closing session looking for her in particular. When Evelyn refused their invitation, as she later told her, Dr. Livingston, always the psychiatric grandstander, said he would talk with them and went along to the Thames House.

Earlier in the day, Michael had forwarded a BBC broadcast alerting people to these dangerous "waking dreams." The government's Minister of Health told people to suppress them like bad thoughts or daydreams since they could lead to "mental instability." And they should immediately see a psychiatrist. The Ministry's website listed doctors across the British Empire, no doubt cooperative ones, including Earl Livingston. He also attached links to coverage of how yesterday's BBC report had created a global media sensation, with outlets from Algeria to Brazil and all across Europe and the U.S. reporting on this phenomenon. So the shit had indeed hit the fan, and she wondered if that was for the best.

Of course, conspiracy theorists worldwide had a field day, especially those who felt the COVID virus was a depopulation ploy by the Elite. The pervasive theme was that this psychic outbreak was a government conspiracy to control our minds. Several theorists claimed to have had one of these "waking dreams" and did bizarre things like trying to drive into the CIA compound in Langley, Virginia, and getting arrested. While these themes dominated the internet conspiracy sites, some mainstream television reporters contacted and interviewed people who had actually had this experience; some felt it had put them in touch with God. Of course, even these sincere and mostly credible accounts were treated with equal disdain by the government-controlled media mavens.

Today, Maria had gotten several calls for appointments from people having waking dreams. This outpouring caught her off guard, and tomorrow she planned to write a topic paper and post it on her website for people to digest before scheduling an appointment. Then, Maria heard from Evelyn that British Security had warned her and the BPS about publicly countering the government's health assessment on this outbreak. Privately, doctors could say what they wanted to their patients, but since the government called it a public health hazard, they couldn't contest that publicly or face the consequences. While the government had allowed some debate over the COVID vaccines, they claimed this was more critical. Evelyn said they were really panicked.

But outside of her shared dreams with Catherine, which had become more periodic since they had dropped their therapy sessions, Maria had not yet had one of these waking dreams. She did not see the "lighted lady" vision at the Jung symposium. Also, Cat had not taken her on an excursion into the Collective Self, if she could call it that, like with Alicia Holmes and others. That woman was now more of an ally than an adversary, and maybe SPS's Greg Mires too. Maria wondered if her reluctance was due to some innate resistance or a psychological block, but Cat assured her that they needed an objective observer at this stage. At least, Maria told herself, she didn't feel compelled to follow Cat's path to celibacy if that held, which she doubted. Today she had invited Michael over for some "hot sex," which should clear her energy field, she thought. He was more than willing and would bring Thai takeout for dinner.

After Michael arrived and they were eating their meals, he asked, "So we're not having any more death dreams."

"Not since the dinosaur dream with Cat."

"I think the Brits might be onto something, and I plan to suppress or ignore any such dreams that show up."

"Maybe you should come to the office for a session."

They finished their dinner, and Michael picked up the cartons and threw them in the trash. "Doctor, the only session I want with you is horizontal, not vertical."

She laughed. "I hear you, Big Boy. And I'm all for that."

They had hardly made it to the upstairs bedroom pulling off their clothes along the way until they flopped down on the mattress and made love. Within minutes, they approached explosive orgasms. Then, suddenly, *they were in a dream state with hundreds and then thousands of couples worldwide having sex and all coming simultaneously. This group orgasm seemingly shattered the barriers between them as they merged into a collective postcoital state full of love and light. Heads now turned here and there, crossing boundaries and viewing others in their collective. This seemed to move everybody into a higher, more cohesive state of being. Then, one of them said,* an East Indian, *"Let me introduce you to Tantra,"* which he then explained."

This collective outpouring made it easier for Maria and Michael to follow these instructions. It soon opened them up to an influx of what the man had called "rising kundalini energy" that just suffused them and was like nothing they had ever experienced. Afterward, Maria saw that Michael had been "touched" as he tenderly kissed her and went to sleep. His spiritual opening held out real hope for their relationship. After gathering herself, Maria went downstairs and called Catherine to share this experience.

The woman gasped, "Well, I think I better call Stephanie and experiment with that."

Maria smiled. "How convenient for you."

16

Saint-Tropez, France

Stephanie was sitting on the balcony of her hotel overlooking the white sand beach and the azure blue waters of the Mediterranean, drinking a glass of Chardonnay. It had been a hectic day at the magazine's bikini photoshoot at Tahiti Beach. Then, her phone chimed, and she was about to ignore it as she always did on location. There were too many horny men looking for hookups that no longer interested her. But she sensed this call was different and glanced at the Caller ID. It was Catherine.

"Hey, sweet thing. What's up?" Steph asked.

"Just wondering if you're in town and if I can come over."

"Cat, you're welcome to fly to Saint-Tropez; you'd be better company than some of the dweebs hanging around here." She paused. "Or, maybe you could just pop in."

"I was thinking of something more physical." She told Steph about Maria's experience and the seemingly global orgasm she and Michael had experienced.

"Wow. That does sound euphoric, all right. But my focus is elsewhere these days. I mean, I've had waking-dream connections with at least ten people here in the last two weeks: some models, actors, producers, and makeup artists. The encounters leave me . . .

ecstatic. And when I run into them in person, they've changed, and we connect more deeply. It's hard to describe."

"Tell me. Try illuminating fifty shrinks at a Jung Symposium."

Stephanie sighed. "Doesn't sound very appealing."

"It at least got some of them out of their heads." Cat paused for a moment. "Wait. I feel something coming on. Let me see."

Catherine now appeared in Stephanie's hotel room. First, the model called down and canceled her room service. After they caught up with each other, the two formed an energy vortex and were soon joined by some of her recent dreaming friends in what Cat later described as an astral get-together. It was a transformative experience for all. Afterward, when Stephanie went down to the restaurant for a quick meal, she noticed that some of the people she passed in the hallways, the lounge, and the restaurant seemed affected. There was a soft glow around them. Did their vortex energy permeate the whole hotel? She took her time eating her vegetarian fare and watched everyone closely, but the effect didn't seem to wear off. Back in her room, she called Catherine, and they explored the possibility, like with Maria and Michael's global orgasm, if this wasn't a faster way to spread the light. Cat heard from her father that their initiation had affected some neighbors, including Uncle Henry.

The photo shoot ended in a few days, but Stephanie stayed behind for some vacation time, as she told everyone. Some of the others who had been connected in their vortex energy experience stayed as well. While remaining isolated in their hotel rooms, the group got together and started creating more energetic outreach gatherings. Media commentators soon talked about how peaceful it had gotten at the beach resort and that the party and the bar scene had practically disappeared. How everything was just "lit up." This calm was so unlike the city at Christmas time. Catherine had joined their group at their last session and showed them how they could become attuned and spontaneously reach out to others in these waking dreams, then draw them into "get-togethers." One participant into Transcendental Meditation told how back in the 1980s, TM groups would descend on a city and mediate for a month lowering the crime rate there. This exploit sounded similar to theirs but on a global basis.

San Francisco, California

Catherine picked up Stephanie at the airport's international terminal and drove to a restaurant in San Bruno north of the airport to meet Maria for dinner. This location was still southeast of the city proper, and nobody should notice Taylor there. Of course, they were both anxious to get back to Stephanie's house in San Rafael for a vortex group exploration, but that could wait. They ordered first, and all declined alcoholic drinks.

Maria had never met the model and wanted to get to know her first before they delved into their other concerns. Stephanie had never gone to a psychiatrist, despite her childhood abuse. After some probing by Amidala, it became apparent that the woman needed some psychiatric analysis.

"Yes, I'd like that, but I'll have to say that with each dream experience, especially the group get-togethers, stuff seems to come up, and something shifts. For the first time, I feel like talking with my Dad, maybe giving him a chance to say he's sorry about what happened."

"That's wonderful, Stephanie. But you might wait until we have a session or two to see how resolved the issue is in your unconscious mind. Childhood abuse can leave some deep dark wounds that are not so easily healed." Stephanie nodded her head. "Let me ask, have you had any recent dreams about your father?"

"No, never." She sighed and almost shivered as her eyes teared up. "I guess you're right. Let's do that, Dr. Amidala."

"Call me Maria outside the office."

"Okay, Maria." She paused and lowered her voice. "Cat has told me that you've held back from the actual waking dream experience as an outside observer." Maria nodded her head. "How long will that last? I mean, it seems like the more evolved group participants have the greatest outreach and impact in our gatherings."

She was saved from answering this inquiry by their Chinese dinners being served. In a sharing mood, they placed all three meals in the center of the table and everyone helped themselves. After that, the conversation turned to more casual inquiries. Stephanie entertained them with some of the mishaps at her recent photoshoot. In one incident, a sudden wind storm blew her bikini top out to sea at a remote location, and she just continued the shoot using splayed fingers to cover her breasts. The magazines were getting more risque, as seen by the latest *Sports Illustrated* calendar issue.

They finished dinner, sat back, drank green tea, and read their fortune cookies. Nothing on point, however. Finally, Maria said, "I was thinking, especially after my global orgasmic get-together with Michael and the others, that it was time for the next step. So, why don't you come back to my place, and if you're in the mood, we can do a group dream session there."

Catherine reached over, took her hand, and then looked at Steph, who smiled. "We'd like that."

They gathered together in the living room at Maria's Twin Peaks duplex, sitting on cushions with scented white candles providing the light. Since Maria had yet to participate, Cat and Steph would first create the vortex and see if she was drawn into it. Once formed, like an internet chat room, others pressed to join in, but their hosts waited, and then Maria appeared. People associated with her who had had waking dreams were now showing up, like Michael, much to her delight. This included a U.S. senator she knew and a foreign trade rep from Japan. The vortex grew larger until Catherine had to close the entrance gate but allowed one last participant, someone everyone knew from his TV appearances. The interchange of these more evolved and somewhat older individuals brought the two young women to a higher level, but their energy also infused them and awakened their vital energy bodies. While engrossed in the experience, Maria could see the energy cords forming between people and wondered if this was a means of further transmission to others.

Afterward, Cat and Stephanie were too wiped out to drive home. So they spent the night in Maria's spare bedroom. That led to the bonus of a shared dream between the three of them. They soon found themselves running on the beach at Saint-Tropez until they flew off into the sky toward the stars.

Kemerovo, Russia

Elena was sleeping in Inna Kuzmin's bedroom. She had a large bed and room in her chest of drawers for her friend's clothes. At first her father, Sergey, was alarmed to have a renegade FSB officer in his home. But after dinner that first night and a private talk in the living room, he changed his opinion, especially after the man showed him pictures of his wife and daughter. The whole family had been affected by Inna's dream life, and if Elena was as important as his daughter had claimed in spreading this energy and this officer was here to protect her, so be it. He could sleep in their son's bedroom in the basement; Damir was away at college in St. Petersburg and wouldn't be coming home anytime soon. His scholarship didn't cover long-distance travel.

Over the last couple of months, Elena had dream experiences with hundreds of people, primarily children but some adults, around the globe. As they reached out to others, their circle grew rapidly. Now, it was just more convenient to have shared group dreams with everybody. At first that became a bit chaotic, but an organizing energy, what some of the children called God but that Catherine explained in psychological terms, seemed to integrate them. Either way, the experience had changed all of them, and the wider it spread and the more people brought into their circle, the more powerful it became. They had learned that you couldn't talk with adults; you could just bathe them in the light and let them find their way back to their core center.

Elena was concerned about the soldier woman, Galina Ilyin, who had met with her at school and had sent Kostya to bring her to Moscow. She couldn't just tune into people, read their minds, or do any of the standard psychic intrusions, or not yet. However, after an initial experience of physical or spiritual contact, she could appear in a waking or nighttime dream as she often did. It was as if an energy cord formed between people after the first episode, and when they connected to others, those cords were a conduit for her and others. But this outreach did not apply to physical contact. Kostya had told her yesterday that there was an FSB search for them and that they had to stay indoors and not contact anybody, like her parents or her teacher Arina. But Elena sensed the goodness in Officer Ilyin and wanted to connect with her.

She had tried a dream incursion into her FSB office in Moscow. But the building's energy was so dense that it blocked her intrusion, or it did for now. Maybe if she could shift Officer Ilyin out of her mental state, the woman could start working on them. Possibly stop their search. After the officer's work on Friday, Elena showed up on the train while the woman was riding the underground metro home. It was later than usual, and her compartment wasn't fully occupied, with only a few commuters at this hour. Galina looked up from her cell phone and saw Elena in her dream body sitting across the aisle. This apparition startled the woman. She looked around to see if anybody else could see the girl but apparently not. She could now hear a voice in her mind.

"I hope I haven't caused you any trouble, Officer?"

The woman put her hands to her temple and then understood they could talk telepathically.

"No, but we are concerned about you. Did you force Officer Stepanov to hide you?"

"No. Once Kostya touched this energy, he wanted to help."

"Elena, the two of you must come in now. You are a priority target. It's not safe for you."

Elena closed her eyes and let the energy between them intensify, fed by these light streams. Galina caught her breath and said, "Oh, my God." The woman next to her scooted farther down the bench. *She then let the energy waft through her. It brought up and started healing wounded parts of her. The woman now understood what was at stake for her people and others across the globe. She opened her eyes.*

"So, Elena, what do you want me to do? Stop my investigation of you and the others? That would compromise me."

Suddenly, Kostya showed up sitting next to Elena. "No, continue investigating but cautiously. Your presence there and your contact with others will help change the situation. You can't talk them into compliance, Galina, but just suffuse them with this energy. Trust the inner voice."

"Well, Stepanov, if this energy can crack a hard nut like you, I guess there's hope for the rest of us."

Kostya added, "That includes your father but don't share this contact with him yet. Your energy will do what it can do, and he'll find his way back to it.

Suddenly, they disappeared. Galina just shook her head clear but felt amazingly elevated. Then, finally, the woman on their bench seat said, "You seem out of sorts, young lady. Maybe you should see a doctor."

"No, I'm all right. Much better now."

Elena came back while sitting in the chair in their bedroom. Inna was lying on the bed, her head propped up by a pillow.

"Good visit?" she asked.

"Yes, the FSB woman. I think she's with us now."

"As are some of the local police. My Dad's been very helpful. A policeman who saw the wanted notice asked about the strangers in our house. Dad dream-connected with him, as others call it, and the officer has buried the notice."

"Let's go to sleep and dream some more."

"Yes. This dreaming is like a global sleepover."

17

Teen activist Lexandra Berg had had waking dreams with a Russian girl for the past month. On her first appearance at the apartment, Lexi, as everyone called her, was, if not alarmed, surprised by this apparition. But, having provoked the ire of many world governments with her environmental campaign and having received death threats from conservative groups, she was as "tough as nails," as an American advisor had said. She then proved that by walking across a bed of red hot coals for the media. Lexi could feel the girl's high energy and soaked it up. With each exchange with Elena coming here and her going there, she felt softened up or better in touch with deeper parts of herself and others. Lexi now understood the broader consciousness picture. She had been trying to convince people of the rightness of her ecological cause, but she was learning that words alone directed at the ego-mind could not move the greater populace. The change had to come from within them.

It took her a while to understand how this energy worked, how it permeated people, and how it could be "broadcasted" or sent out from her energy field. She first tried her experiment on a small group of nonsupporters. Lexi brought them into a room and gave a talk from a podium, but like Elena and the American Catherine had shown her, she brought forward her dreaming body, and that light energy seemed to waft through the group. Some of them closed their eyes and let it activate them at the deepest levels of their being. Others were oblivious to this outreach. One person jumped up and hurried out of the room as if, in his mind, demons were chasing him.

When they brought Dr. Richardson into their media plot, she opposed it. Repressed people might fight the energy and become compromised. So Lexi called upon that higher aspect of herself, what Dr. Amidala called the Self, to mitigate any harmful effects of this outreach. The energy had already backed off from the unreceptive, but it now seemed more sensitive. She tried a larger test group, and while many people weren't affected, nobody had an adverse reaction. Lexi wanted to wait until late January to give her speech, which was the anniversary of the disastrous Gulf War Oil spill of 1991, but Catherine convinced her to do it in the next few weeks, given the growing world crisis.

She picked Stockholm University as the forum since it had one of Europe's best Environmental Science programs. The auditorium was filled with students and activists from around the world. Her people had alerted the media that this would be a groundbreaking speech, and all the international networks were covering it. Catherine, Stephanie, and other vortex group leaders meditated and bolstered Lexi's dreaming energy body. Only minutes into the speech, moans and sobs could be heard from the audience. Cameras moving across the gathering found some people with closed eyes and euphoric facial expressions as if experiencing something deeply profound. Then the cameras came around and focused on Lexi, who seemed to have white light around her, like the iconic pictures of Medieval saints. Maria and Catherine could see streams of light beams pouring out of her.

Many viewing the speech on television or over the internet and even later watching a rebroadcast seemed affected. A scientist in their group said the effect was nonlocal and that time or distance wasn't a factor, like with precognitive waking dreams. After the speech, some affected news commentators uncharacteristically dropped their neutral global warming stance and called for governments to act on this environmental disaster before it was too late. Swedish Security Service, SÄPO, brought Lexandra in the next day, accompanied by her lawyer. When they asked her about the extraordinary spiritual reaction to her speech people worldwide were having, she just told them, "Consciousness is contagious."

"What is that supposed to mean?" asked an acerbic interrogator.

Her lawyer Gretchen Carlberg said, "It means, if you don't get it, we can't explain it."

With that, she ushered her client out of the office and back to her apartment. The two of them then joined the dreaming get-together of her key supporters worldwide. "No politics tonight," one of them said, "let's just spread the light far and wide." So they drew in Catherine in San Francisco, Elena and Inna in Siberia, and the many people connected to them. Since they had figured out how to move this revolution, if you could call it that, globally and not just person by person, the organizers were thinking of ways to reach out to politicians and industry giants or the world's movers and shakers. But, of course, they might not be as open to this expansion given their investment in a corrupt financial system. Hopefully, their affected children would eventually elevate them.

Two weeks later, as Lexi was driving out of her apartment building's underground parking lot, Elena appeared and told her to return home. She said that bad people were waiting for her outside on the street. Lexi backed up into her parking spot. In her apartment, she called her contact at the local police station, who dispatched squad cars to this location. They found two suspicious parked vehicles with criminal types. Suddenly, as if provoked by a threatening presence, the men jumped out and ran across the street. This maneuver was enough of a provocation to stop them. They were all carrying guns, illegal in Sweden, and taken into custody.

The police did ask Lexi if she spotted the suspicious cars coming out of the garage. She did, and they told her to keep a watchful eye. The men were taken to the local police station. Finally, one broke under questioning and claimed that Russian agents hired them to kidnap Lexandra Berg. This confession immediately brought SÄPO into the investigation. The Russian contacts were identified as SVR and GRU agents, which led to a formal protest by the Swedish government.

It also brought a female security officer to a meeting with Lexi and her lawyer at the girl's apartment. Before she arrived, Lexi contacted Catherine and was told to share more about their outreach. The officer, Errika Lingren, showed up with a policeman who waited in the hallway. Lexi served them tea with rye crispbread wedges, and then the woman addressed the issue at hand.

"Lexandra, or can I call you Lexi?" Errika asked.

"Please, just Lexi," she replied.

"I was in the audience at the university when you gave that speech, and while I was not as affected as some, I could sense certain energy in the room. And by all accounts, people watching the broadcast were similarly affected. Can you explain that?"

Lexi looked over at Gretchen, who nodded her head. She turned back to the security officer. "In the last few months, I've had what you could call a spiritual awakening. No particular religious sect, just a feeling of how we humans are all connected at a deeper level, a group soul, as someone said, and I've learned to go to this place full of light and spread its energy. I did that with my speech, but I was as surprised as you by its pervasive outreach effect. Even people just watching it on TV seemed to be affected."

Gretchen simpered at this minor deceit, then added, "I think that explains this spiritual effect."

"Thank you, that was quite illuminating, as they say. But why would Russian agents want to kidnap you?"

"The Russian media, in a country known as Europe's gas station, has vociferously opposed Ms. Berg's environment stance, especially regarding the burning or use of fossil fuels," the lawyer added.

"I see. So it's not only this spiritual effect, but you stirring up environmental protests? If not broadcasted on Russian television, Lexi's speech was on the internet until they blocked it. But we've heard people downloaded it and sent clips to others via email blasts. And people marched in Moscow on the environmental agenda. Risky for them."

"Surprising, given the general repression there," Gretchen added.

"Indeed," Errika replied.

Back at her office, she wrote a report about this meeting and gained insights. It quickly went up the line to those in charge. Her report led to a global inquiry about this "effect" with other security forces worldwide, and a response from MI6 led them to Gerald Harris at MI5. He told his SÄPO contact about waking dreams and their agency and the American's concern about its rapid spread. The next day, Lexi was assigned a police detail. Gretchen had to wonder if it was to protect or contain her.

Moscow, Russia

At the SVR's First Directorate Headquarters in Yasenevo, Deputy Director Ira Savin was reading a report about the failed abduction of the Swedish activist Lexandra Berg. While SVR agents were only indirectly accused of the exploit, his superiors blamed him, even if the GRU conducted the main operation. Another "clusterfuck," as the Americans would say. Last week the FSB Director, Grigori Tarasov, reported that Berg's speech, while blocked on Yandex, if not Facebook at first, had gotten out and affected people across Russia. His task force leader, Galina Ilyin, and her staff had interviewed people who watched the speech and had a religious renewal. While Russia wasn't as crazy about such movements as the Chinese, Tarasov's concern, rightly so, Savin concurred, was that this waking dream phenomenon was now spreading rapidly.

His secretary, Daria, announced, "Major General Tarasov and Lieutenant Ilyin are here."

Savin moved around his desk to the round conference table, and when the FSB Director and his science officer stepped inside, he showed them to their seats across from him. Daria asked if they would like coffee or tea, but they declined.

"I assume you heard about the abortive kidnapping in Sweden yesterday?" Savin asked.

"Was that the SVR or the GRU?" Tarasov asked.

"Russians either way, but my superiors, in the wake of this embarrassment, are asking was the kidnapping necessary."

Tarasov, who wanted to spread the blame, turned to Galina. "Tell him your assessment, Ilyin."

"So far, this waking dream effect has been spread from person to person. However, we've interviewed people who also claim to be drawn into, what can I say, some kind of ethereal get-togethers."

"Damn. That doesn't sound good." Galina nodded. "Go on, Officer."

"But, if someone can spread this energy via the media and over the internet, it's another level of concern. This activist has one of the largest followings on Facebook and other worldwide social media outlets like Instagram. So while we scrubbed her speech here, her presence is spread all over these outlets. Maybe her mere presence on a site passes it along. You can't close down everything."

"And you didn't see this coming, Lieutenant?"

Galina paused. As her father had once told her, "Never accept responsibility for a botched assignment; they'll just go down the line to blame someone else."

"No, sir. Not knowing the true nature of this phenomenon, how can one judge how it will spread?"

"So that's the real problem." Savin paused. "We need to bring in one of these perpetrators."

Tarasov asked, "What's happened with your search for Elena Mongush?"

Galina could see where this was leading. "As you know, I had an agent at the FSB regional officer, Kostya Stepanov, pick the girl up to fly her to Moscow for just that kind of inquiry, but they both disappeared. We have a national police search that hasn't turned them up yet. No signs of their immediate families either."

"So she 'affected' the officer?" Savin asked.

"Yes, that's our best guess, and someone equally affected must be sheltering them."

Savin sat back in his chair. "Damn. This thing is getting out of hand." He picked up a TV remote, turned on his television, and panned to a saved video. "This was a British national broadcast by their Health Ministry." He played the translated broadcast for Tarasov's benefit. "Is it at that point, Lieutenant, where we should do the same?"

"Sir, I'm not sure, but the effect, whatever they claim otherwise, could make people less complacent."

Tarasov nodded, liking her careful wording of the general effect. He exchanged looks with Savin. They had something planned.

"This is not just our problem, but it's spreading worldwide and is becoming a major security threat to all nations?" Savin asked.

He looked to Galina, and she nodded her head.

"I agree, Ira. So you think we should reach out to the Brits?"

"That's what I'm thinking, but we can't make this a high-level inquiry from the two of us, especially given the current tension between the West and Russia."

"What do you suggest?" Tarasov asked, following the script.

"I'm thinking Lieutenant Ilyin, heading our internal Waking Dream Task Force, should make the inquiry." Savin paused and looked at Tarasov. "Before the tension gets worse."

They both turned to Galina. She had seen this coming. "I could, but I need an official SVR or FSB authorization document. I mean, given our tension with the West."

"Of course, Lieutenant. But, given the global threat of this psychic virus, I guess you could say, maybe we should reach out to other countries as well."

"Yes, sir. I think that's called for," Galina added.

"Good, Lieutenant. Give me a moment alone with Director Tarasov?"

Galina gathered her valise, stood up, and stepped out of the room.

Savin turned to Tarasov. "Is this woman that savvy, Grigori? I mean, asking for documentation."

"Her father, who lives with her, is ex-KGB. So it either runs in the family, or she's been coached by him."

"Either way, I'll generate the document and provide the contact information, and from what I'm getting from the Kremlin, I'll make it fast."

"The timetable has been moved up, Ira?" he asked.

"Let's just say we're under the gun to resolve this before the inevitable onslaught."

"Agreed."

18

Washington, D.C.

General Morton had been to the White House numerous times, but this was the first visit for Alicia Holmes. As they drove past the iconic white building on Pennsylvania Avenue, they saw groups of protesters carrying signs on the sidewalk: "Waking Nightmares," "Tinfoil Hats for sale," "Another Viral copout," "Psychic BS."

Morton shook his head. "This could get as bad as the COVID protest."

"But it won't kill them," Alicia said.

"Yeah, but most of them would rather die than change."

Alicia looked over at the General and wondered if he belonged to that group.

After they drove to the side entrance and passed their screening at the sentry gate, Morton parked in the West Wing's private lot. A Secret Service agent met them at the side entrance and took them to the offices of the National Security Advisor, Preston Gates. They waited in his reception area for thirty minutes and passed on drinks offered by his secretary.

"General, do you know the NSA?"

"Yes. I dealt with Gates when he was part of the Obama think tank. Bright guy. A Harvard man."

"And you Yalies talk to this guy?" she simpered.

The General laughed. "You bet. He backed us to the hilt on Neptune Spear."

"What's he like, if I may ask?"

"The Brits liked him because he was a Rhodes Scholar. Cerebral. Probably too much of an egghead for my taste."

His secretary heard that description and smiled. Finally, they were ushered into his office. Gates was a tall man in his forties with thinning brown hair who looked more like a college professor than a security maven. He was standing at the window looking at the protesters outside the WH iron fence and turned to them. After Morton introduced Alicia and gave him her background, Gates looked over his shoulder. "I hope you can tell me what this outpouring is about. I mean, this waking dream syndrome just jumped out of nowhere."

"Yes, sir. I believe we can." Gates ushered them over to his small conference table.

"I guess this has something to do with why Secretary of State Erwin Parker had a . . ." He looked down at his notes. "'Spiritual awakening' and yesterday turned in his resignation to the President." He paused. "I was told by the Secretary of Defense, who attended yesterday's NSC meeting, that you may be able to shed some light on this phenomenon and his behavior."

Morton gave the NSA a rundown on their investigation of how people getting touched by this energy have had what they call an awakening to humanity's "dire situation."

Gates just shook his head. "Jesus. Not something you can wrap your mind around. Might have to bring my wife in on this one."

Neither of them commented. Finally, Morton told him that the Brits and the Russians have been following this development closely and that it may indeed be a matter of National Security.

"So somebody remote-views someone, I take it, or shows up in your space, and you go wacko?"

Morton turned to Holmes, who said, "Sir, from our investigation, I wouldn't characterize them as wacko, and it only happens if you're susceptible to the energy. It seems like they get in touch with some kind of Collective Self, as the Jungians call it, and experience an emotional uplift and a spiritual awakening for some."

Gates nodded his head. He had a psych minor in college and could understand the jargon. "You say the Russians are on to this development?"

Alicia added, "As best as we can tell, a ten-year-old Russian girl was the first to have these waking dreams. At first, she had precognitive visions of things yet to happen, and then she showed up in some kind of dreaming body and affected others. She lives in Novosibirsk, Russia, the home of . . ."

"The Russian parapsychology experiments in the 70s and 80s."

Morton added, "Her grandfather was Dr. Yuri Mongush of the military unit 71592."

"Are you saying this is some kind of delayed holdover from the Russian mind-control experiment from that era?"

Morton shook his head. "No. The Russians, given their state-controlled regime, are even more alarmed. And when the FSB tried to pull her in for questioning, she disappeared with an agent sent to escort her."

"Okay, this is now on my security radar, despite the crazy protesters. But let's get back to Parker. I assume it's too soon to understand where this leads people, but is there any hope of bringing him back to the land of the living?"

Morton looked to Alicia again. "I would have to talk with him; I've had this experience, and while it's affected me, I have a broader perspective on it."

Morton was startled by her admission, and Gates chuckled, "But I shouldn't expect something popping out of your chest like in the movie *Alien?*"

Alicia laughed. "No, sir. This is strictly a human experience, spiritual, but nonetheless disturbing for outsiders."

"The Secretary is at Walter Reed for observation. If you're up to it, Ms. Holmes, I'd like the Secret Service to take you there now and have you meet with Erwin. Hopefully, to talk him down."

She looked to General Morton, who nodded but still had questions. Alicia turned back to the NSA. "Has a psychiatrist been assigned to him?"

Gates shrugged his shoulders. "I've not been following it that closely, but if so, I'll clear the way for you to talk with Irwin in private."

They now stood up. "General Morton, if you could stay behind, there's another matter I'd like to discuss with you."

"Yes, sir."

IT WAS A FIFTEEN-MINUTE DRIVE from the White House to Walter Reed. Alicia was escorted to the psychiatric ward. She waited for thirty minutes before a doctor in a white coat came down the hall to her. He looked down at his iPad.

"Doctor Holmes, is it?"

Alicia stood up and shook his hand. "Yes, in psychology, and you are?"

"Dr. Truss. I've been told to give you access to Secretary Parker, although I'm still unsure why?"

172

"It's a matter of National Security, as the NSA's people should have told you."

"Yes, I am aware of that, but that doesn't allay my concerns."

"Sorry, doctor. I've been told not to discuss this matter with anybody else and that I would have unfettered access to the Secretary in private." Truss nodded his head and started to escort Alicia down the hallway. As they walked, the doctor keyed up the room's camera feed on his iPad and turned it off.

"Has he been given any medication?"

"Just a mild sedative. Secretary Parker was brought in yesterday, rather docile and cooperative, and slept well last night. Actually, he doesn't seem to have any behavioral problem that I can see, but my access has been limited."

They now came to a suite where a military guard sat outside. "Ben, this is Dr. Holmes, the NSA had given her clearance to meet with the Secretary."

"Yes, sir." The man opened the door and announced their visit. Parker was sitting up in bed reading a book.

"Secretary Parker, this young lady, Dr. Alicia Holmes, has been cleared to talk with you by Preston Gates."

The tall, gray-haired African American slid off the bed, stood up, and shook Alicia's hand. No fist bump. He then escorted her to the room's table with its two chairs. Dr. Truss shook his head and left.

"So, Dr. Holmes, are you a super shrink or a military assassin here to do me in?" he asked with a smirk.

Alicia smiled and looked over at the older man. "No, sir. I guess you could call me a fellow contactee." This designation startled the man.

"I assume we're not talking about ETs, but the Vortex Energy, as this Catherine Dumont calls it." He looked up at the camera in the corner of the ceiling.

"I was assured that this is a private conversation, and I know Dumont, and she has taken me on a journey to what she calls the Collective Self."

"Oh, my God." Tears welled up in the man's eyes. He closed them. "The light, the light was overwhelming." He opened his eyes. "I've just had a couple of contacts with her and others, and then these group get-togethers in this etheric realm, as she calls it." He shook his head. "You know I am what you would call a Southern Christian, if a bit lapsed, but this is like being in the presence of . . ."

"God," Alicia said. Parker nodded his head. "And you found it hard to just go back to work, given all the toxic energy inside the Belt."

"Yes. In another context, an earlier generation has said, 'How Ya Gonna Keep 'em Down on the Farm After They've Seen Paree?'"

"The task is how do we bring more people to Paree."

Secretary Parker added, "So you think I should resume my duties but with dreaming contacts to . . . refresh the fount, as it were, when needed?"

"Yes, Mr. Secretary. Your mere presence at this level will have a beneficial effect."

"Call me, Erwin, Dr. Holmes. And let's work that out."

After an hour of conversation, Alicia knocked on the door, and the Secretary's military guard opened it. She asked him to call Dr. Truss.

Minutes later, the psychiatrist showed up. "Good meeting?"

"Yes. And Secretary Parker is ready to resume his duties but refuses to undergo any psych evaluation."

"I don't think that's possible."

"He said you'd say that, and if the Secretary needs to, he'll talk with the President."

Truss swallowed hard. "That won't be necessary."

London, England

Galina Ilyin flew into Heathrow on a military jet and was met at the private terminal by SVR Agent Vlad Petrov from the Russian Embassy. One of the new breed of foreign agents, he was educated at Oxford and Georgetown in Washington and spoke perfect if British-accented English. In his mid-thirties, he was blond-haired and fit with light intelligent eyes. In the limousine drive to the embassy, Petrov looked over at Officer Ilyin. She wore civilian clothes on this foreign mission—a blue skirt, a pearl-colored blouse, a light green jacket, and a gray wool overcoat. Her English, if not perfect, was passable.

"Is this your first visit to England, Lieutenant?"

"Yes, but I've watched my share of BBC detective stories set in London."

"With your father, Fedor? I believe he was stationed in London during the Cold War."

She smiled at his evident background search. He probably knew what kind of chocolate she preferred. "Yes, he liked their Beef Stroganoff with the thicker Crème Fraiche, as he supposedly told my mother on his return, but he didn't like the fried foods."

"After stints in the U.S. and here, I've gotten more accustomed to that, but I draw the line at Scottish haggis made with sheep heart, liver, and lungs."

"That doesn't sound very appetizing at all. Thanks for the warning."

Petrov nodded his head. "As far as warnings go, the tension between our countries couldn't be worse. I'm amazed they agreed to meet with you over such an odd concern."

"Agent Petrov, you've been briefed about these waking dreams and how they are affecting people worldwide?"

"Just enough to know it sounds pretty sci-fi to me, but the Brits certainly have their *knickers in a knot* over it."

Galina laughed. "I've not heard that expression. But nobody, as we Russians would say, is *making elephants out of flies* on this concern."

"Can you give me a more thorough rundown on it?"

"Sorry, Officer, but I've been told only to share information with the embassy's SVR Rezident."

"You mean my boss, Maxim. Good luck with that. He's what the Americans call a meat-and-potatoes type of guy."

When they arrived at the Russian Embassy in Kensington, Maxim Romanov, a short man with gray hair perfectly cut, asked Galina if Petrov could sit in on their briefing. "He's Western-educated, and maybe he can make some sense out of this situation because it's beyond me."

"Yes, sir. Whatever you say."

Romanov moved them to a small table where his secretary served them dark tea from a porcelain pot and set down a tray of Russian tea cake cookies. She then left and closed the door behind her.

Galina gave the two of them an abbreviated briefing on the "waking dream" phenomenon and its inception by a ten-year-old Russian girl in Novosibirsk. She told them that the SVR had learned this is a priority for the English and American security services. However, what has alarmed them, since until now its spread has been a person-to-person transmission, was Lexandra Berg's speech that seems to have transmitted this energy over social media sites and affected people in Russia and around the world.

"This is some kind of psychic virus that's influencing people, giving them spiritual experiences, and possibly making them politically noncompliant?" Petrov asked.

"Yes, Officer. We sent the resident FSB agent there to pick the girl up and bring her to Moscow for further study, but they've both disappeared."

Romanov asked, "And the British are ahead of us on this development and consider it enough of a threat to share with us at this contentious time?"

"Yes, sir. You might have heard their national broadcast and waking-dream warning."

"That was rather astonishing." He paused. "Okay, I see the danger here. But I'm going to contact Savin and ask him if Agent Petrov can accompany you to this briefing since, as the Germans say, *I only understand train station.*"

This familiar European idiom drew polite laughter from the two agents.

Romanov took them to dinner with his family at Mari Vanna in Wellington Court. It was like eating in a traditional Russian home with its nesting dolls and ornate chandeliers. Maxim seemed more at home here than in his office and proved to be an entertaining host. His wife, Kira, a large Slavic woman with coiffure blond hair and bejeweled, kept trying to fix her up with Petrov, but neither was interested if Galina did recognize his "openness."

The following morning Officers Ilyin and Petrov arrived at MI5's headquarters at the Thames House in Millbank. There was a great deal of tension in the air. They were met by an underling, Officer Ronald Davies, the assistant to Gerald Harris heading up this inquiry for the Brits. He was gracious enough, but on their initial eye contact, Galina could see that he was one of them or an insider with dreaming experience. He took them to a formal conference room where they met Harris while MI6's liaison to the task force stood back and was not introduced.

First, there was a little grandstanding by both sides, or between Petrov and Harris over the current crisis, until Galina stepped into the fray. "Look, both our countries and maybe the whole world is at risk from this . . . social development. Let's get to it and figure out how we can better manage this situation."

Harris nodded his head. "One of our so-called dreamers, the Russian dissident Makarov, had his Kremlin episode while off his antipsychotic medication clozapine, and none since being put back on it."

Galina nodded. "Thank you, Mr. Harris. That is helpful. Have you tried to prevent such dreaming in others with this medication?"

"No. It's been too early, and once people have had this experience, they aren't very cooperative."

"Yes, that's been our problem, too. We can't investigate something without test subjects. We tried to bring in Elena Mongush, but she has eluded us."

Davies looked at Harris. They had inadvertently identified a local Russian contact where she might be holed up, but Harris shook his head.

Galina saw that exchange. She added, "But this person-to-person exchange of . . . energy, and even these etheric group get-togethers is one thing, but our main concern is how Lexandra Berg's speech carried over social media had something of the same effect, if not as powerful."

There were a few snickers from the other side, no doubt aimed at the SVR's abortive kidnapping attempt. Petrov caught this undercurrent and quickly offset it. "Look, we are all at risk. But our three countries, including the Americans, have the best scientists in the world, so why don't we start there? Create an exchange between them to fix this problem."

Harris tapped his ear-comm. Apparently, he got approval for this venture from the higher-ups. "Okay, I agree. So let's work out the protocols."

Petrov looked to Galina as their emergent science officer to lead the way, but she shook her head and deferred to him. *Let him knock heads with these spies*, Galina thought. She also realized it was much too late for that kind of intervention. The Cat, literally and figuratively, was already out of the bag, as the English say. This psychic virus had spread even faster than COVID. Governments had a lot of handwringing on how this could have exploded so quickly, but it seems to have struck a deep chord in people looking for renewal, psychological or spiritual.

After working out a mutual arrangement on the science exchange, Petrov dropped Galina off at her hotel. On the drive over in the limousine, he studied her closely. Finally, he asked rather provocatively, "So how does this feel?"

"Excuse me, Agent Petrov. What do you mean?" she asked, looking into his eyes.

"You've been investigating this contagion from the beginning. What are the reported effects to look for in others?"

"It varies, but those open to it seem to feel connected to something beyond their egos, something transcendent." Galina watched Petrov's reaction, more inviting than off-putting. Interesting.

"I see. My sister would like that, but then she's the crazy one in the family."

When they dropped her off at her hotel, Petrov stuck out his hand. Galina looked at him. *Why not,* she thought. Galina shook it, passed him the energy, and hopefully woke him up. He smiled back at her.

That night she had a dream exchange with Officer Davies. He told her that Elena Mongush might be hiding out in Kemerovo, Siberia. Galina did not share this information with her superiors upon arriving home in Moscow.

19

Mill Valley, California

Catherine had the week off between Christmas and New Year's but started her vacation a week earlier. Soon she had the house to herself. After Jeff's split from his girlfriend, which he took very hard, he decided to spend time with his family in San Diego. And Stephanie was off to Dallas for a family holiday reunion, the first in years. Maria invited Cat to dinner with her and Michael, but she declined, wanting to stay alone. Or, as she asked herself, if that was possible with all the near-daily dreaming connections? She had discovered that intent was the key to that, and if disinclined to connect at any given time, it closed the "gate," as it were. She was amused by her central position in this global awakening, as one of Lexi's supporters had called it. From a quiet mouse a few months ago, as she liked to call herself, she went from there to an internationally known facilitator of this dreaming energy. What had happened to her, or how was she so quickly drawn into this worldwide campaign?

As with her waking dream at the Jung Symposium, appearing as an iconic feminine figure ablaze in light, she had not consciously willed it but followed the flow of energy and its use of her. In a sense, Cat guessed she was a consenting adult, as they say. But the effect of this dream energy was that her boundaries were getting blurred or coming down. It wasn't as if she heard the sound of a thousand voices like you see in films about psychics, despite her early dream of seeing a thousand faces in the carnival mirror, maybe a precursor of sorts. Instead, it impacted her more at a feeling level or feeling the distraught emotions of the people she just passed on the street or those seen on live broadcasts on television. She had brought that up with Maria; her advice was just to let the feelings run through her, and eventually they would self-integrate, and they did but also kept coming.

Then, she heard a call on television for volunteers at several soup kitchens in San Francisco, which are hectic during the holiday season. She thought about it, but did she want to expose herself to the heightened emotions of street people who flocked there during the holidays? Maria advised against it, given her lack of feeling boundaries, as she characterized it. But, again, Cat found herself following the flow of her dreaming energy and its outreach and called some soup kitchens, one of which was run by the sister of a work colleague, where she volunteered.

She dressed warmly and fully covered with her dark wool pants and hip-length violet sweater, and as advised, her blond hair was tucked under a blue watch cap, and she showed up early on Christmas morning. Catherine quickly got to work with the rest of the volunteers. First came baking the whole chickens and turkeys in the ovens, then later she chopped vegetables and the meats for the giant vats of soup. Next came peeling and boiling the Idaho potatoes, then mashing them and siphoning off the chicken and turkey juices for the gravies.

By noon they were ready to set up the buffet and open the doors. There were pans of chicken and turkey pieces, someone carving a whole turkey, huge vats of mashed potatoes, soups of all kinds, piles of buttered biscuits, raw vegetables, and at the end, an apple crisp casserole. Karen Knowles, her colleague's sister, in her thirties with blue-framed glasses and a slick Apple watch on her wrist, supervised the buffet. She had people set behind each offering to scoop the food onto the passing plates. Karen now placed Catherine at the end of the line to serve the apple crisp casserole.

First, she looked Cat over and pushed a strand of blond hair back under her watch cap. "Catherine, I'm putting you here. I'm afraid that if you're farther up the line, the guys will want to talk with you, given your looks, and it'll slow things down."

"Don't worry, Karen. I know how to handle tough customers." She gave her a steely look.

Karen laughed. "Okay, but these people are pretty fragile. Don't scare anybody to death."

Cat nodded as the doors opened, and the first group poured into the banquet hall. A couple of the guys and women stood back to get an overview. One guy, tall and thin, with a scruffy black beard, brown jeans with knee holes, a long wool shirt, and a military cap, picked up a plate and walked straight to Catherine.

"How about some of the apple casserole, beautiful?"

Before stepping onto the floor, she had drawn in some of her dreaming energy, thinking this group needed more than a good meal today. She wondered, given the venue, if she should pass that by touch, despite the now-loose COVID restrictions on hand contact. It was worth a try. Cat looked at this guy with her kind eyes. "Why don't you start with some nutritious food first?"

"Looking at you is all the nourishment I need."

She reached out and just tapped the man's hand to energize him. He shuddered a bit and then stepped back. "Sorry, ma'am. You're right; I'll start at the front." He turned to walk away.

"That's good, Handsome. I'll save a big scoop for you."

He smiled from ear to ear and shuffled away. In the background, Cat spotted a twentysomething black man, casually dressed in clean dark clothes with intelligent eyes, watching this exchange.

The pace picked up, and plate after plate got large servings of her casserole from the stainless steel container. As expected, some men and women stopped to ask her questions since this was her first time at the shelter.

One of the women, a bit portly with dirty stringy brown hair, asked, "Seems like you'd have better things to do on Christmas than cater to us down-and-outers."

Catherine looked at the woman, and in a flash, something relatively new for her, she saw her long and tattered history. It started with childhood neglect, intermittent schooling, bad jobs, and worse boyfriends. She put down her scoop, reached over, and took the woman's hand. They both closed their eyes with this exchange of energy that almost overwhelmed her.

Finally, the woman opened her eyes and blinked repeatedly. "Jesus, lady. That's one hell of a charge you carry. Are you a healer or something?" She paused. "If so, give me a card."

Catherine added, "You just got my card, Missy. Tune into it."

The woman was about to ask how she knew her name but was pushed along by the next person in line. Afterward, Cat looked up as the line thinned out, and she found Mr. Clear-Eyes still staring at her. Then, finally, he got in line, and by the time he reached Catherine, nobody was behind him.

He stared at her, and she looked back at him. "I'll take some of the apple crisp and a whole lot of that energy you're sharing, Missy."

"Catherine or Cat." He nodded his head and introduced himself.

She reached out her hands. He took them, and they both closed their eyes, but here was somebody ready to take a full load, and she laid it on him. He practically shivered as the light permeated his body. Then, she opened her eyes and saw the dark splotches in his aura start to clear up as the light dispelled some of his negative energy.

He pulled back his hands. "I saw the government's broadcast about these waking dreams and their dangers, and I wonder if you aren't one of the perps."

She scooped a large portion of the apple crisp onto his plate. She then added, "And now, Andrew, you're one of us. Pass it along."

"You've got it, Cat." He picked up on the dreaming energy pretty quickly. And she wondered how some of his friends at the shelter and future contacts would respond.

After three hours, with the next round of diners arriving, Karen gave her a break. They went back to the kitchen, pumped cups of coffee from the lever-action stainless steel container, and sat at a server's table. Someone brought over plates of food.

"So, Catherine. You're a real draw, and I don't mean your fashion-model looks. What's up with you, and will you come back and help us again?"

She reached over and took the woman's hand, and they both closed their eyes. Afterward, Karen felt amazingly refreshed. Cat looked at her. "You won't need me. You're the conduit now."

San Francisco, Tenderloin District

After lunch at the homeless shelter, Andrew Houseman walked around the Tenderloin district to let the energy flow through him from his encounter with Cat. He would've walked to the San Francisco Museum of Modern Art on 3rd street if it were opened today. He was an aspiring artist, more pop than fine art, and loved the art displayed there, especially Mickalene Thomas's acrylic, enamel, and rhinestone collages of African-American women. He had talked with her at a recent exhibit there, and they had hit it off.

It had been a rough two years for him, especially during the COVID crisis, when he lost his part-time job and apartment/studio. But, unlike some down-and-outers here, he had not resorted to drugs or crime to keep going. He attributed some of that inner stability to his mother, Gwendolyn, a medium and spiritual healer. While she was no longer on this plane, as she would call it, he could feel her presence around him and almost see her shaking her head if he indulged in lowlife behavior or got depressed. While he felt alienated from her Christian God, who seems to have deserted him and his black race, he believed in Mama, the House, as people called her.

As he walked along, Andy could imagine that in other, more well-to-do areas of the city, the streets would be deserted on Christmas as people stayed home, ate their big family dinners, and opened their elaborate gifts. Unlike some of his brothers, he did not resent or decry "white folks" because, as Mama would say, "The same God that animates them flows through us. Condemn them; you condemn Him." But, unlike his mother, he could separate the soul from people's minds and their egos. Today, after his healing or whatever happened at the soup kitchen, he was in love with everybody he passed on the mean streets of the Tenderloin. He said his hellos and got waves and greetings back from them. It wasn't as much the Christmas spirit; it was Mama's, or maybe Cat's, energy flowing through him and connecting with people.

He found a bench and just sat there all afternoon, watching people pass by and sending the downhearted a little love. Andrew was more liberal than his mother, and while he occasionally read

Mama's Bible, he also read books from other spiritual traditions. He remembered reading one by this English teacher, Eckhart Tolle, talking about doing the same thing early in his awakening, just sitting on a bench and watching people and quieting his mind. Finally, Andrew headed back to the shelter for dinner and his army cot for a good night's sleep. While he ate a meal with his friends there, he was in his own space, not that anybody was aware enough to notice it. Finally, the lights went out, and he slipped beneath the covers of his cot and quickly fell asleep.

He wasn't much of a dreamer, but he dreamed of Catherine tonight. She came to him in a loving outreach and showed him how to call up people on an inner screen. He followed her instructions, and soon there were hundreds of people in their little squares, not photos of them but live images—all of his friends at the shelter still sleeping appeared there. Then the screen expanded, and he pictured people from his past still alive and others he didn't even know in other city shelters here and elsewhere.

Cat showed him how to tap these images with his now-lighted fingertip. Some of the squares lit up, and they looked back at him from their dreamtime and sighed as the energy around them changed while other picture blocks went black. He sensed that this was the dreaming energy he had heard about and that Cat had imbued in him. It felt amazing, like pure love—or the closest he had experienced with his mother and his younger sister Magdalene or Matty. She had rejected Mama and her Christianity, but she suddenly appeared in her lighted block, looking back and sending him her love.

This experience lasted longer, but he didn't remember much more. Then, waking up early the next morning, he opened his eyes. A few men from the shelter, who had responded to this dreaming energy, hovered over him. It was as if to say, "What's up, Dude." They all appeared energized and more grounded, light without feeling flaky. Andrew smiled and sat up in bed. "What's up is that you guys are next, and here's how it works." He gave them Cat's activation instructions, and they returned to their cots. They now used their dreamtime to pass along this energy to family, friends, and even foes.

Andrew got dressed, picked up a paper cup of lukewarm coffee from the kitchen, and headed toward a friend's art studio that would soon open, as he was an early riser, too. Bobby let him set up his easel and acrylic paints in a corner. As Andrew walked along the streets with a few stars still blinking in the early morning sky, he thought of Van Gogh's *Starry Night* with its swirling energy vortexes and felt inspired to create a collage along this line. His *Starry San Francisco,* with its swaying office towers and their blinking lights like stars and with swirls of energy around them, would soon launch his artistic career.

20

Hong Kong, China

While banned in mainland China, Facebook can still be accessed in the *special administrative regions* of Hong Kong and Macau. That's how radio talk show host Bai Jin saw Lexandra Berg's environment rebroadcast from Stockholm. She had watched it several times and felt deeply affected by the environmental issues, such a pressing problem with China's coal-burning utility plants. But she was even more affected by the so-called "dreaming" energy people talked about on social media. Bai was a yogi and a meditator and could feel the transmitted spiritual energy. She had friends going to college in San Francisco who spoke about the global sensation caused by Berg's broadcast. They mentioned a local Bay Area woman, Catherine Dumont, as an advisor to Berg. The Chinese censors were particularly sensitive to religious movements. Everybody knew of the suppression of Falun Gong and the religious practices of the Uighur Muslims and others. So she was reluctant to email friends about this dreaming energy. But she knew from her metaphysical studies about "calling up" people in her meditations.

After a late-night Saturday radio talk show broadcast, she shut down her computer and meditated. She called out to Dumont by name and location and patiently waited for a response. None came after an hour, and so Bai went to sleep. But she dreamed of a blond-haired woman who said, "You called?" She asked "Cat," as she referred to herself, about transmitting this light energy in her broadcasts to Hong Kong and the mainland. Bai was shown how to draw the dreaming energy into her body and use her voice as Berg had as a conduit. She didn't need to talk about spiritual topics, and the more banal the exchanges, the better. But people listening and open to it would absorb some of the energy, if not as potently as from a live TV broadcast like Lexi's or direct contact. That was even better; she didn't want her listeners getting too charged up, just more aware.

It took several weeks of dreamwork to settle the energy into her body. After several people at the studio remarked about how charged-up she seemed recently, Bai had to contain her expansive energy. And then, on a late-night show, she could feel it seep out as she talked with people about practical concerns. Bai had a degree in psychology from the Chinese University of Hong Kong and could deal with most people's complaints about infidelity, relationship problems, and general issues. However, she had a firm policy restricting political questions or concerns—one reason her radio show was broadcasted throughout China. Then, a week later, came the litmus test question.

"Bai, I've listened to your show for years, but just recently, you seem charged with a different kind of energy."

"How's that, ma'am?" She had a no-name policy as well.

"I don't know. But I asked you about my husband's drinking two weeks ago, and while your advice was, what can I say, pretty standard, he started to drink less even though I had not brought up the issue with him again."

Bai waited a moment, let the energy settle in her, and chose her words carefully. "Sometimes, it is the changes in us that change others. Maybe after years of listening to me, you've become a better listener. People just want to be heard, and he might drink to quiet angry voices or complaints you're more willing to hear now."

The woman chuckled. "Maybe, but I still think something is happening with you. Got a new boyfriend, Bai?"

"No. My Welsch Corgi Ping gives me all the love I need."

The woman laughed. "If you say so, my dear."

While social networking was banned in mainland China, no Facebook or Instagram, the government allowed professional associations, and Bai was a member of a national broadcasters' group. They held annual events in either Beijing or Shanghai every year. Given recent political restrictions in Hong Kong, she thought it best not to attend this year's gathering in Shanghai. But they did put out a program with the names and faces of attendees from around the country. She knew many of them from past gatherings.

Following Cat's advice, she printed out a color program with the photos of those attending this year's annual meeting. Studying the pictures before she went to sleep, she had learned how to pull up a screen with their photos and tap the blocks with a lighted fingertip. Most of the blocks went dark, but dozens more lit up. Nobody could trace this activation back to her. But, without Facebook or even Google on the mainland, she wondered how they would connect to Catherine or hear Lexi Berg's speech and get a further renewal. However, she knew from her Qigong teacher that spiritual energy would find a way to express itself to everyone's greater benefit. "You just had to be prepared to answer the call."

Bai had kept up with the pro-democracy movement in Hong Kong since it boiled over in 2014, although she had not made a public display of her support. Media stars like herself were closely watched, and those who crossed the red line, as they called it, were censored, and some lost their jobs. One prominent pro-democracy reporter had been jailed this year along with the more agitating proponents. Last year's overhaul of Hong Kong's legislature, with the minority share of seats directly elected by popular vote down to 20 from 35, and even those candidates vetted by Beijing, created a violent reaction. Fifty-three pro-democratic activists and former legislators were arrested in last January's crackdown. She was saddened by what might happen to them in prison.

While Bai supported the pro-democracy movement, she couldn't lend her voice or donate money to the cause. Some friends from her college who had gotten caught up in the protests had urged Bai to speak out. Some even tried to breach the subject in call-ins to her talk show. From the start, her producer had introduced time delays for callers. They were screened for arrest records and topics to discuss. Given her show's popularity and its outreach to the mainland, this made Bai unpopular with some local activists, even though she was promoting change in another undetected way. But she had also denied an interview request from one of Hong Kong's prominent legislators, Guo Wang, who later started her own radio talk show to support the political clampdown from Beijing.

Fortunately, the list of current legislators, along with vetted candidates for the next election, was readily accessible online. Bai was encouraged to follow the energy that might lead to waking dreams with those she had had contact with over the years, but she felt that would be too provocative for most of them. Westerners didn't get the strained political atmosphere here. She did pull up a screen in her dreamtime with these people; some of the pro-democrats lit up, but none of the others. It was a start, and she would keep at it. Then, Bai was invited to a cultural event, an exhibition of a public art installation, very modern and contemporary, showing the blending of virtual and physical reality at the Hong Museum of Art.

Guo Wang and her politically correct entourage were there to show their liberal streak. Bai liked the exhibit and had to agree, given her dreamtime activity, that the lines were indeed blurring. She walked around and talked with people, especially the artists in their colorful punk outfits. At one point, Wang came over and asked how she liked her talk show.

"As you know, Madame Wang, I'm not very political, and the discussions don't . . . move me."

"Bai, whether you like it or not, we live in the real world, not the virtual wannabe world of the protesters."

Bai took her hand. "Are you sure about that?"

Wang reacted to the contact and pulled away. "Wow, hot hands. Have you been juggling any hot potatoes lately," she said, snorting and walking off.

"We'll see, Madame."

Bai could feel the transmission of the dreaming energy and watched Wang as she went back to her group. She now held the hand of a young Chinese man, Li Wu, her Western-educated media coordinator in his late twenties. He was taller than average, handsome, and very bright, then Wang rushed off to the bathroom. How interesting.

LI COULD FEEL SOMETHING pass between Guo and him as she held his hand and urged him to circulate among the guests. "Don't be shy, Li. You're my media star. Connect with people," she said; he wasn't shy but bored at such media functions. He preferred being the director, not the actor.

Suddenly, Guo looked down at her hand. "My hand is really hot. I wonder if Jin has COVID and passed me the virus. Excuse me. I'm going to wash my hands. You should, too, Li."

"Yes, ma'am."

Guo looked back at him and shook her head. "It's Guo. I'm not your mother, Li." She laughed flirtatiously and headed off.

He took a few steps toward Guo's retreating figure, then stopped. Whatever it was, he liked the feeling, and he was fully vaccinated, as his friends say in the States. Li stepped over to the bar, got a glass of club soda, then strolled over to one of the black leather lounge sofas and sat down. He closed his eyes and could feel this energy coursing through his body. It felt good, not toxic. Li opened his eyes and saw Bai Jin walking toward him. Earlier in the year, he had tried to place Wang on her show, but she refused, saying she didn't do politics.

Jin had smiled at him at the time, and he sensed she did do men. Too bad she was off-limits because of her stance—not pro-democratic, but not pro-government either. She sat down next to him.

"I saw Guo rush to the bathroom. Is she all right, Li?"

"She thinks you passed her COVID and went to wash her hands."

"But you didn't."

"I'm not germophobic," he said. Bai kept staring at him, and it made him uncomfortable. She must've sensed that and stood up.

"Okay, we wouldn't want you to pass any germs to the uppity-ups in Beijing next week."

That was rather provocative, and how did she know about their trip? Li stood. "Enjoy the party, Bai." He walked off.

Guo now stepped over to him. "What did Jin want?"

"Bai said don't worry. She's fully vaccinated."

Wang held her hand up. "It's not hot anymore." But his was.

Several nights later, after this energy had settled in him, Li had a dreamlike encounter with Bai while sleeping.

She asked him how he was feeling.

"Why? Am I supposed to feel different?" he asked.

"No, just more yourself."

"Interestingly enough, I had that feeling today, like I felt unburdened by my responsibilities and was more freewheeling as an assistant said."

"Yes. Not so uptight, so controlling," she added

Then she touched him, and he felt an almost ecstatic charge run through his body.

Li then woke up; it was the middle of the night. He got out of bed, slipped into a black silk robe with its embroidered red tiger, and headed to the floor-to-ceiling window overlooking Victoria Harbour. He often felt guilty living in this expensive high-rise with so many homeless people living on the streets who couldn't afford the city's high rents, even for "closet sleepers." As an old girlfriend once said, his family was well-to-do, political mucky-mucks. Li was educated at Stanford in the U.S. and still had friends in the Bay area. Now that this country was the enemy, he had to cut some ties there. The funny thing was, he felt freer in the U.S. with all of its social chaos than he did here in his controlled communist country, although Hong Kong was freer for now.

His cell phone rang. He had to keep it on all night since Wang hardly ever slept and was prone to late-night business calls, but he wondered about that excuse. Few people had his private phone number, certainly not Bai Jin, whose name came up on his Caller I.D.

"How did you get this number?" he barked.

"The same way I got into your dream, Li."

"And how did you do that?" he asked and sat down on a sofa.

"It's called dreaming magic."

"What? Like shared dreams? I've heard of them from friends in the States. I'm not impressed."

Suddenly, Bai appeared in his apartment as a blurry image. "Are you impressed now?"

He was shocked and had to calm himself. "Okay, I saw Berg's speech and heard about these waking dreams on Facebook. So that was what the hot hand at the museum was about?"

"Yes. An invitation, but you can decline as Wang did."

Li closed his eyes. He could feel the intense energy rise in him. Could sense its possibilities. He opened his eyes. "What is it you want?

"It's about your trip to Beijing."

He nodded. "Of course it is."

21

Arlington, Virginia

General Gordon, three of his SPS scientists, and Director Black-man sat at a conference table in a DARPA laboratory. They viewed a video screen where a woman with electrodes attached to her head sat in front of a monitor playing Lexandra Berg's environmental speech. While this continued, Adam Campbell, bespectacled with dark straight hair, a scientist specializing in subliminal audio/video transmissions, stood next to the screen with the remote.

"We collected two dozen volunteers who had not viewed or heard Berg's speech. We then played the video, and in ten percent of the test subjects, we could detect subtle changes in their brain waves but could not identify any carrier wave."

He clicked his remote, and a diagram of a human brain came up. Then, he brought up a diagram of the right and left cerebral hemispheres; the next slide focused on the right brain with an arrow pointing at an indentation in a brain fold.

"Simultaneously, the right cerebral cortex, involved in intuition, imagination, and feelings, among other functions, was activated in those affected, and there was a lessening of stress throughout the body. When asked, some said they had a euphoric feeling. They were given MRIs afterward and a week later."

He paused and turned to his audience. "Both British and Russian scientists had the same result with their Berg subjects. And, I might add, the Russians were more invasive. Of course, films with imaginative or emotional stories also affect the right brain, if not to this extent. However, even a week later, the brains in this activated group still showed a subtle alteration in the gray matter, an extra fold, which we assume is permanent."

Campbell clicked his remote, and a video of young David Bernard appeared on the screen. He, too, had electrodes attached to his head, drawing a vigorous protest from the scientists. A female psychologist sat across from him and asked questions.

"With his father, Major Bernard's permission, we interviewed his son, who has had several of these waking dreams. First, we did an MRI and detected a similar and larger permanent alteration in his right brain. He claims to have been contacted by this Russian girl Elena Mongush. We asked him to use a waking dream to connect to her, but he told us that it happened spontaneously, at least on his part. We doubted that but couldn't force an activation."

He clicked on another screen showing the psychologist, Margret Whiteside, undergoing an MRI. "However, afterward, Dr. Whiteside experienced some emotional and physiological effects. Her MRI revealed activity in her right cerebral cortex. But again, we could not detect any energy exchanged between them. The next day we sent in another psychologist while monitoring her live brain wave readings, and she wasn't affected, nor did her MRI show that change."

Campbell stepped over and took a seat at the head of the table. "From a scientific point of view, there are signs of a subtle transmission in the activated cases, but we could not detect the medium. We assume with David Bernard that it wasn't a voice transmission since it was minimal, just his proximity to Whiteside."

Morton asked, "Did you pull in anybody actively transmitting these waking dreams like Catherine Dumont?"

"We asked, but she declined an interview or examination."

Morton looked at Director Blackman. "No, Stanley. We can't compel her participation. The British could and had psychologists interview several dreamers with the same variable results. The Russians only know of one Primary, the Mongush girl, who is still at large."

Both of them looked to Dr. Greg Mires, head of SPS. "The Brits brought in Dr. Richardson and could compel her to disclose her research. She claims that the effects are nonlocal in the case of the Russian girl's precognition or her seeing things in the near future. However, in Berg's case, even weeks after the speech, this energy seems to have the same nonlocal effect without a carrier wave, as if people were activated retroactively and tuned into the original broadcast."

Campbell looked confused and added, "You mean like quantum entanglement?" Mires nodded his head. "But that's based on prior contact, like subatomic particles created simultaneously and separated but still linked."

Alicia Holmes said, "Yes, but in terms of Jung's Collective Unconscious, we are all linked at a deeper, fundamental level. The One Soul concept. Or we are quantumly entangled in your terms."

Mires added, "That's the explanation for precognition and telepathy and other such effects at a distance and with nonlocal time lapses."

Campbell shook his head. "I'm a scientist, not a parapsychologist."

Morton looked at Blackman, who spoke up, "Thank you, Dr. Campbell, for your thorough examination. We'll take it from here."

The scientist clicked off the monitor, gathered his things, and left the room. Morton now asked, running his hand through his gray hair. "So, after weeks of study, the conclusion is that we can't stop these experiences from happening?"

Mires quickly added, "As a psychologist, I would qualify them as spiritual in nature. And, so far, none of the major proponents, besides Berg's benign environmental stance, have an agenda. Hers is quasi-political at best."

Morton asked, "Okay, but what happens after millions of people have them? Will they feel above the law or outside of its rule? Compliance with our laws is the lifeblood of our democracy."

Alicia added, "Well, there's the biblical quote: 'Render to Caesar the things that are Caesar's and to God the things that are God's.'"

Morton spitted back, "Need I remind the two of you that our mandate is to protect our country and its people, and I'm still not convinced this isn't a threat."

"I'm sure that's what the pagan Roman Emperors said about those quirky Christians until Christianity became the state religion," Alicia said.

Morton glared at her. "Alicia, given your own dream experience, you might recuse yourself from this investigation."

Alicia replied, "General, as the Jungian would say, my experience adds a balancing element, or it's compensatory to the general assessment." He looked less than convinced but backed off.

Greg hurriedly turned to Eric Darby. "Eric, you've initiated a public opinion poll of those affected. What's the verdict there?"

"I added some hot questions like, 'Does your waking dream experience agree with your faith?' 'Will you stop going to church?' 'Does it change your political views?' 'Does it make you closer to loved ones?' First, a number of people in the U.S. have had an experience along this line so far—mainly via Berg's speech—and over 90% of them claim that it was positive. Some even said it put them in touch with God."

Morton shook his head. "But does it change their politics?"

"They say they'd like more honesty and better values from politicians."

Blackman laughed. "Yeah, me too."

"So what do I tell the people at the DOD who report to the president?"

Mires slid over a recent Washington Post article. "The Secretary of State claims to have had waking dreams, and it made him a better Christian."

"Look, everybody, you know that these Black Swan events or movements are totally unpredictable. And I agree with MI5/6 and the Russians that this needs further study, and we will push forward with our investigation."

Morton gathered his valise, stood up, and left the room in a huff. The SPS contingent looked baffled. Then, Blackman added, "Remember, the General saw something coming, if not this. Stanley's trained to identify a threat and then contain it as a military man, but there's nobody to fight here. It's like trying to bag a ghost."

"Yes, Director." The four of them stood up and walked out of the room. As Mires and the others took the elevator down to their floor, Eric joked, "I wonder which flavor of Kool-Aid we should drink at lunch today?"

Alicia snickered. "How about *Tropical Punch* since we just got bitch-slapped."

Mires shook his head. "Come on, Alicia. Just roll with the punch."

She punched Greg in the arm.

When General Morton stepped out of the DARPA building, he saw a government limousine pull up to the front door. He stepped over to the young driver, who powered down his window. "Who are you picking up?"

The man looked up at the General's uniform, then down at his clipboard. "A Major Bernard and his son David."

"Taking them to the airport?"

"No, sir. Secretary Parker wants to take them on a tour of the White House."

"Damn." The General hurried to his car. He got in and took out his cell phone. Morton put a call through to the WH switchboard that forwarded it to National Security Advisor Preston Gates. His secretary answered.

"I'm sorry, General. But the NSA is in conference with the Secretary of State."

"I know what they're talking about and have updated info they need to hear."

"One second, sir."

A moment later, Gates came on the phone. "What is it, General?"

"I just came from a briefing at DARPA about Major Bernard's son, David, suggesting he's a propagator of the dreaming energy we talked about. And now Secretary Parker wants to give him and his father a tour of the White House? That's highly questionable."

There was a long pause. Morton could hear Gates discussing this reservation with the Secretary. "How far out are you?"

"Fifteen minutes."

"Okay, get here and join the discussion."

When Morton stepped into the NSA's office, he found Major Bernard and David sitting in the reception area. Bernard stood up and saluted him.

"At ease, Major. I hope you and your son enjoy your stay in Washington."

"Thank you, sir."

Morton turned to Gates' secretary. She stepped over and opened the door to the inner office. Inside, Secretary Parker stood up and stuck out his hand. Morton hesitated.

"Don't worry, Stanley. I'm not contagious." He fist-bumped him.

"Have a seat, General," Gates said. Morton pulled out a seat at the mini-conference table. The NSA was reading a report on his laptop. "I called Blackman and had her forward DARPA's early assessment report." He looked over at Morton. "If I understand the implications here, David Bernard's mere presence can trigger this dreaming energy?"

"One of the two psychologists interviewing him was affected." He paused. "As were ten percent of the test subjects reviewing Berg's speech."

Parker chuckled. "Hell, one in ten in a general population is nothing, and in these circles, we're pretty buttoned-down, Stanley."

Gates looked at his laptop screen. "Your guy Mires says they are spiritual experiences?"

"That's a broad category. Schizophrenics have spiritual experiences."

Parker added, "But President Lowell and his staff have entertained the Dali Lama and the Pope." He grinned. "Didn't see any conversions there, but then the President has been wearing more red ties these days."

Morton shook his head and turned to the Secretary. "Mr. Secretary, this is still an unknown contagion if I may characterize it as such. We wouldn't subject anybody here to a smallpox carrier."

Parker shook his head. "Really, Stanley. My experience of it was quite illuminating. You should let Alicia pass it on to you."

This suggestion only made the General clench his jaw.

Gates pushed his chair back. "Secretary Parker, this phenomenon is still a possible threat. For security reasons, I will have to ask you to forestall your White House tour. Take the Bernards to the Smithsonian, buy them dinner at a swanky restaurant, and then put them on a plane."

Parked nodded his head. "Okay, while I think you're overreacting, it's your call." He stood. "Stanley, at some point, we'll have to live with this awakening. And you should switch your focus from containment to management." He turned to Gates. "Preston." He then walked out of the office.

Gates looked at the General. "Stanley, if I may suggest, let's go forward with both containment and management strategies. And I'll need more hard statistical data. At some point, we will have to brief the President."

Morton stood up. "Okay, Preston. I'll follow up on that."

Gates stood and shook the General's hand. "And don't let Parker throw his weight around. This situation remains a national security matter."

"You've got that right."

General Morton walked to his car in the West Wing's private lot. As he drove through a light drizzle to his home in Stone Ridge near Dulles Airport, he wondered about his assessment of this dreaming energy threat. It was definitely a Black Swan event, but so were the internet and personal computers, and they had benefited humankind. He was a lapsed Southern Methodist who believed in God and country but was also a nuts-and-bolts military strategist. In the field, you don't let wishful thinking or personal prejudice muddle your thinking. But, since Greg, Alicia, most of his SPS crew, and even Secretary Parker thought that this development could have a positive effect, that was now the lay of the land. Adapting, adjusting, and figuring it out was this soldier's mantra.

He used his car phone to call SPS and was routed to Greg Mires. "How did it go with the NSA, General?"

"Fine. Look, we're also going to devise a management strategy for this dreaming energy outbreak. So get your people working on that this week. And Greg, I'd like you and Alicia to come to my house for dinner on Saturday." He paused. "And, yes, I know about the two of you, and I'm happy for you. Just want to look at this in a relaxed family setting."

"Sounds good, General. We'll be there, and thanks for the invite."

"My son Brad's home from MIT. Ask Blackman if they have any hypersonic test vehicle models for him. He's in aerospace engineering."

"Yes, sir. I'll do that."

AFTER A FESTIVE DINNER on Saturday, Stanley ushered Greg and Alicia into his private office. They had all declined after-dinner drinks and were ready for a serious discussion, or so the two of them thought.

Morton started, "Look, I'm not what you would call a free thinker. As an army general, I think about contingencies and force applications." He paused. "I know, way outside your realm of concerns. But I'm also a realist and know when my history or personal orientation acts as blinders on a critical security issue."

The two smiled, and Alicia knew to relieve the man's uneasiness. "General, would you like us to share this 'dreaming energy' with you, as we've been calling it?"

He nodded his head. "I need to experience what I've been called upon to manage."

The two of them moved over to the sofa and sat on either side of him. They each took one of Morton's hands. "Close your eyes, General, and release any anxiety about this experience. It's pleasant and illuminating."

General Stanley Morton closed his eyes and, after a minute or two, found the white cord of energy that led him to what his Methodist Minister would call "The Godhead." He let out a deep sigh of relief. He somehow felt whole again.

22

Vatican City, Rome

Papal Emissary Father Dante Belmonte was picked up at the Leonardo da Vinci Airport by a limousine and driven on the Autostrada Motorway to Vatican City. It was a 40-minute drive that gave Dante time to gather his thoughts and settle his energy to report his findings to Cardinal DiNapoli, one of the Pope's senior advisors. He had been dispatched by the Cardinal, the most liberal of the Pope's inner circle, to investigate what was being called "dreaming visions of God." Dante was chosen for this assignment because of his Oxford education and his Ph.D. in psychology. The Vatican was first alerted to this phenomenon by Jesuit psychiatrist Dr. Mateo Russo in London. After a Jung Symposium, he filed a report about such visitations. It claimed that people worldwide were having these visions, which interested them. But that levelheaded Russo, along with others at the symposium session who had a vision of what he described as a "Blessed Mother" image, was galvanizing. While the envisioned woman, Catherine Demonte, wasn't even Catholic, her associate, Dr. Amidala, was, if lapsed.

Russo had met him at Heathrow for the fifteen-minute train ride into London. Sitting in an open car, they did not have enough privacy for even a preliminary discussion, so they talked about world affairs and the tension between the East and West. In the city, Russo took the prelate to an old English tavern for lunch. Having visited the city often during his years at Oxford, Dante felt at home and even ordered the working-class meal of pie and mash—a minced beef pie and mashed potatoes. Russo ordered the hearty oxtail soup, served with lots of stewed vegetables in a bouillon broth. They drank hot tea, Earl Grey.

After the waitress had served their tea, Dante looked over at the psychiatrist. "Really, Mateo, the Blessed Mother." The Jesuit described the full-of-light image people saw at the symposium and what it evoked in him, if not its actual appearance. He further elaborated on the general discussion about these waking dreams and their association with the Self. Dante was familiar with Jung's interpretation of the psyche. At one point, he had thought of becoming a psychologist and would've been a Jungian. But he felt a more profound spiritual commitment to God.

"Many of my psychiatric patients are having these visions, a kind of remote view of other people's lives at first, and then for some later, a deep inner spiritual connection. As a result, they are getting more integrated if not instantly healed."

"How's that?" Dante asked.

Russo gave the priest the background discussion at the symposium that these "waking dreams" were directed by the Collective Unconscious or the Collective Self of humanity. "I don't know if you read my Ph.D. dissertation, but long ago, I associated Jung's Self with our Christian God. He later even characterized the *objective psyche* as a self-conscious force that nurtures the development of the individual in their quest for self-actualization or illumination, as God and his minions do."

"I recall reading that and thinking the same thing, Mateo."

"I brought up Jung's quote at the session about 'being gripped by something that is stronger than myself, something that people call God.'"

"I imagine that went over well."

"Yes, with the customary snickers and rolled eyes, and then the waking dream of Dumont, as she gradually became filled with a light that seemed to fill the room, stopped them cold."

"Interesting. Did everyone there see it?"

"No, and it seems to have deeply affected only some of us."

"Good. So it's volitional and not forced."

Russo nodded his head. "Yes, and from reports on the internet, that's a key factor with people accepting this dreaming energy, as it's called, or not."

"Yes, but Cardinal Rizzo would say, 'The devil works with his pleasant enticements.'"

"There is evil in the world," Russo added, "but I would think we prelates have gone beyond those Old Testament fears."

"Christ showed us how the Love of God conquers all, but in matters of faith, I like to fall back on the old Russian proverb, "Trust but verify."

Russo laughed. "Yes, I'd say they at least got that right."

Their food was served, and they ate for a while before resuming their discussion.

"Dr. Richardson, an English psychiatrist and professor at London University, a crusty old bird, as they say, is Dr. Amidala and Dumont's contact here. I tried to arrange a meeting with her, but MI5 intercepted the phone call and told me she was off-limits for now."

"Wow. So the security agencies have stepped in rather quickly," Dante said in amazement.

"Yes, including SVR/FSB, since the initiator of these visions seems to be a ten-year-old Russian girl in Siberia." He paused. "She has apparently gone into hiding with an FSB officer sent to escort her to Moscow, or so I've heard from my government contacts. Most distressing for them, I would think."

Dante nodded his head and continued eating. This discussion was getting very interesting. Finally, he asked Russo, "Can the Apostolic Nuncio make an ambassadorial request for access to Richardson?"

"I asked the Ambassador. He made inquiries but got the same response and recommended we drop it for now."

"And the Americans?" Dante asked.

"While their government has aired the same cautionary broadcast about these waking dreams, they can't block your access to Dr. Amidala or Dumont by U.S. law."

"And they both live in California's Bay Area?" Russo nodded his head. "Can you check if they are open to talking with an emissary of the Holy See?"

"Yes, I know Maria Amidala from past conferences. I'm sure she'll see you, but Dante, I have to warn you about Dumont. They say just being in her presence can trigger this energy."

Dante smiled. "Let's hope so."

Russo nodded. "'Once more unto the breach, dear friends . . .'"

"'. . . In peace there's nothing so becomes a man,'" Dante added.

"Some men of the cloth might draw back from such a bold venture."

Dante waved the waitress over. "Then, let us drink a pint to stiffen my resolve."

San Francisco, California

The Archdiocese of San Francisco had sent a car for Father Belmonte at the airport south of the city. In a phone call the previous night, the archbishop had suggested that Dante sleep off his long trip here before he meets with these "women." He reminded the archbishop that he was spending the night in New York before continuing his westward trek and would be well-rested for his appointment. The driver, Father Kelley, a young prelate in his early thirties, gave him more background on the doctor and the "questionable" Catherine Dumont. A private detective had uncovered some unsavory details about her.

"The Archbishop is concerned, Father, that they may use the Papacy's interest in this phenomenon to promote themselves and these radical visions." He paused to see if his appeal had resonated with the emissary. No response. He then added, "Or, pass this 'contagion' on to you."

"I'll thank the Archbishop tonight for his concern. But Cardinal DiNapoli and I are both intrigued by these visions of God seen by many worldwide."

"Yes, of course. I imagine it's more authentic than recent sightings of the Virgin Mother in a piece of toast or a grilled cheese sandwich, or is it?" Father Kelley questioned.

Dante looked askance at the prelate. Then, finally, they pulled up to the doctor's brownstone building. "Would you like me to come in with you? I can wait in the reception area."

"No, Father. Just drive back to the archdiocese, and I'll take a cab there later."

Father Kelley started to object but caught sight of Reverend Belmonte's ecclesiastical ring and deferred to him. "Yes, of course. Have a good meeting, Reverend."

Dr. Amidala and Catherine Dumont were waiting for him in the psychiatrist's inner office. Dante bowed instead of shaking hands, and they did likewise. After they sat down, Claire served them Earl Grey tea, set out a plate of cookies, and then left.

Dante added some crème to his tea and raised it in salute. "Earl Grey. I see I'm not the only one doing a background check."

Catherine bristled in annoyance. "I didn't appreciate the archdiocese looking into my sexual history."

Dante set his teacup down and looked shocked. "My sincere apologies, Ms. Dumont, and I didn't request that. I will reprimand the offending party."

Maria asked, "And what is the Vatican's interest in the two of us?"

"Please, we know of your connection to this dreaming energy and the experiences people worldwide are having . . . visions of God, some say."

"That's their interpretation. As a Jungian psychiatrist, I call them visions of the Self."

"Which Dr. Russo has associated with our belief in a Godhead as doing much the same."

"Yes, I know Mateo's view of it. But again, it is just another interpretation."

"Either way, from what I gather in my limited research, it has renewed people's faith in a Higher Power, as the unaligned 12-step programs say."

Catherine relaxed a bit and stared at the prelate and had an intuition. "Oh, you've come to experience it yourself?" Dante smiled. "Isn't that risky?"

"Well, we're in the God business, as someone once said, and if these dreaming experiences bring people closer to their . . . Higher

Power, then we're prepared to, if not endorse the experience, take a wait and see attitude."

Maria said, "That is a rather progressive stance, Father."

"I report to Cardinal DiNapoli, considered liberal within a general conservative hierarchy. But . . ."

"You need to know if its spread is volitional as generally assumed and what the parameters are." Dante nodded his head.

Maria looked at Catherine. "Initially, like mine, these waking dreams, telepathic visions, or even remote viewings as some call them, were of incidents in other people's lives. It was as if some inner force was trying to connect us at a deeper level to break down the barriers between people and maybe races and countries. For some, that's as far as it goes, but for others opened to it, it then connects them to the Source, the Self, God, Higher Power, or whatever, and renews them."

"And how does it get passed on?" Dante asked.

"First, the Russian girl, Elena, would show up as a vision to people and open them up, as it were. Then it progressed to those affected passing it along by touch, voice, inner contacts, or even their mere presence in some cases."

"And people can accept or deny the access?"

"Yes, Father."

Dante picked up his teacup and took another sip. "Then, I'd like to experience that."

Catherine scooted her chair around to Dante's and took his hand. "Just relax, close your eyes, and go with the flow."

After a minute, Dante gasped, "Oh, my God," as he merged with this glowing white light and felt the immense love for all beings of what he considered the Almighty Godhead. Then, finally, after what seemed forever, he opened his eyes and sighed.

THE PAPAL LIMOUSINE pulled off the motorway and made its way through the streets of Rome to the Vatican. Dante's waking dream experience had been overwhelming; for him, it was a direct connection to God or his understanding of the Divine. He would recommend that the Papacy take a wait-and-see attitude toward these dreams while he would expose those opened to it, as Cat had directed him. He knew the Cardinal would be interested, but others would dismiss it as psychic contamination. He could imagine a conclave held to consider this dream state and their visions, but he would advise the Cardinal to experience it before making any decisions.

The limousine dropped Dante off at a side entrance, where the Swiss Guard examined his credentials, even though they knew him, and passed him through. He went to his quarters to drop off his luggage and freshen up. He had called the Cardinal from the airport and would see him an hour after his arrival. As Reverend Belmonte stepped into the Cardinal's austere office, the man in his seventies wearing a red cassock looked up.

"Ah, I can see it in your face, Dante. You're beaming, full of spirit."

"Yes, your Eminence. I believe this may be a way for spiritual renewal, first of the clergy and then their congregants."

"That's more than I expected. So let's talk about your trip, and don't spare any details."

"Let's hope it'll be more than details." The Cardinal smiled. "We'll see."

23

London, England

MI5 supervisor Gerald Harris read the scientific report on the dream transmissions from the tri-country investigation. He shook his head and looked over at his assistant, Ron Davies. "So they can't detect a carrier wave and block that avenue of transmission?"

"Yes, sir. If you read further, our scientists agree with DARPA's, or their subagency SPS's assessment, that it's a form of quantum entanglement and can't be detected or blocked."

Harris said, "That's a mouth full." He paused. "But what about containing major propagators." He looked down at the report. "This Catherine Dumont, Lexandra Berg, and the Russian girl Elena Mongush?"

"SÄPO has put a protection detail around Berg, and just yesterday, Morton has done the same with Dumont, if at a distance."

"General Morton? What, is he switching sides?"

"No, but the U.S. has gone from containment to a management strategy."

"Jesus. They've thrown in the towel already?" Harris shook his head. "The world is going to hell in a handbasket."

"Speaking of which, a Vatican emissary, Reverend Dante Belmonte, paid a visit to Amidala and Dumont." Davies looked down at his iPad and swiped through to a file. "Long-range U.S.

surveillance reported him coming out of her building, 'like he was walking on clouds.'"

"Shit. So the priest got affected too?"

"Probably willingly. I mean, people are having these visions of God."

"Just what we need . . . the Pope endorsing this waking dream spread." Harris sat back in his chair and thought through the situation for a moment. "You didn't mention the Russian girl. Is she still at large?"

Davies scanned through his reports and looked up. "Yes. It appears so."

"Then that's one propagator we can reel in. Didn't our asset, what's his name . . . Dr. Graham, have a patient who identified a possible contact near her home in Siberia?"

He kept scanning through his files. "Yes, a teenage girl in nearby Kemerovo, Siberia, had a waking dream with his patient."

"Before the bigwigs around here cave in like the Americans, call that Russian Embassy attaché . . ."

"Agent Petrov."

"Get him over here. Don't tell him why over the phone, but that it's important."

Davies looked taken aback. "Are you sure about that, sir? I mean, they are the enemy, especially now."

"Not in this battle, Ron. Do it."

Davies went back to his office and shut the door. But before he called the Russian Embassy, he sat back in his chair and "contacted" Galina Ilyin at the FSB through a waking dream. He had passed along that info after their last meeting and now told her that his boss was sharing it with the SVR. She nodded her head and broke the connection.

His request to speak with Petrov was passed through several underlings before the Russian "cultural attaché" came on the line. Then he said that Gerald Harris wanted a face-to-face at MI5.

"Can you just tell me what he wants? I just read the joint science report on these dream states. Not much we can do now, it seems."

"There is something along that line he'd liked to discuss with you."

"Okay, but not at the Thames House." There was a long pause. Then, finally, he mentioned a working-class pub near both their locations in Lambeth.

"Nobody should spot the two of you there."

"That's the point, Davies."

Harris found the arrangement too "lower class" for him, or so he said. It was more likely that he didn't want to get spotted having lunch with an SVR agent. So instead, he sent Davies. When Ron walked into the pub, he saw Petrov sitting in the back and already drinking a pint. He shuffled over to his booth.

"So Harris sent his secretary instead." He stared at the man and smirked.

Davies bristled. "I'm an intelligence analyst, his assistant, not a secretary, and we may know the whereabouts of Elena Mongush."

Petrov gestured for him to sit down. "Okay, we've stepped up our efforts to find her since the conduits, as our joint report calls them, seem to be the only angle left to us now." He held up his near-empty pint glass and pointed to Davies.

"I'd rather not drink."

"Relax, Davies. You're not passing me British secrets, or are you?" He paused and looked over at the man seated a cross from him. "I mean, did you know about this dream contact at our joint meeting at the Thames House?"

Davies didn't respond. "One of our assets, a psychiatrist, had a patient whose waking dream was with a Russian girl, a stripe-haired teenager in Kemerovo, Siberia."

"Yes, in the mountains, an out-of-the-way place, not far from Novosibirsk. And a name?"

"Sorry, that's all we have."

"Okay, it's enough." He looked down at his watch. "It's already 7:00 pm there. I'll call it in later, and the FSB will probably move in tomorrow early morning."

Ron stood up to leave.

"Come on, Davies. Have a pint, eat some fish and chips. Just because our countries act like idiots doesn't mean we need to."

He sat down again. "That's a refreshing perspective."

Their beers were served. They clinked glasses. "To our idiot countries," Petrov chortled. Davies peered at the SVR officer. Yes, Galina had "touched" him.

When the FSB stormed the Kuzman's residence in Kemerovo the next morning, the family was long gone, as was Mongush's family in Novosibirsk, even though the house was under surveillance. Director Tarasov suspected that the family had been tipped off. They must have a mole in the department, and Grigori figured it was Officer Galina Ilyin. Fortunately, their scientists discovered how to identify dreaming propagators with an MRI scan. He now scheduled an "appointment" for her in the morning, but Galina never showed up for work.

Stockholm, Sweden

Lexandra Berg received a strange invitation in the mail: "To meet and discuss her spiritual experiences" with a Crown Princess, the name left off the engraved invitation. She was given the date, time, and room number at the local Sheraton Hotel. Her bodyguards could accompany her to the room but could not come inside. Also, she could not talk about or publicize their meeting. Her lawyer Gretchen Carlberg didn't want her to go and brought the invitation to the attention of her security detail. The day before the scheduled appointment, Errika Lingren at SÄPO cleared it as a legitimate contact, but she wouldn't say who Lexi was meeting, as ordered by her superiors.

For her this screening was unnecessary. Instead, Lexi went inside to her "Source," as Catherine sometimes called it, and it felt good about the contact. When she arrived, the princess's security searched her purse, took her cell phone, and scanned her with an electronic detector wand. Berg's detail waited in the hallway with the Royal's detail. Inside, she immediately recognized Princess Tara, a thin brown-haired woman in her early thirties, who said to call her "Mary, one of a half-dozen names I was born with." She added, "The Royals like to cover all their heritage bases."

Mary showed her to a sofa with a gorgeous view of the city. A tea service was set out on the coffee table, and she poured cups for them.

"You must be wondering about my mysterious invitation, Lexandra."

"Please, call me Lexi." Mary nodded.

"I assume you either attended the event or saw the broadcast of my environmental speech, and it . . . moved you."

"You could say that." She closed her eyes. "Afterward, I had the most remarkable experience. Went to a place full of light and felt loved like never before." She opened her eyes. "I did some research and read about others having this experience. I've also heard that some people become propagators who can share this experience with others."

"Yes, that's happening to some around the globe."

Mary nodded. "You know I'm a member of a very select and powerful group of influential people, the world's Royal Families. I would like to invite those willing to experience this opening and hopefully pass it on. It can only help us all."

Lexi closed her eyes and received strong confirmation. "Mary, we can do that, but I have found that every sharing deepens one's connection to what the Jungians call the Self and others call God. Concerns, habits, and interests seem to get rearranged, as you must have initially discovered. But you have family obligations and will be the queen of your country one day. Are you sure?"

"Lexi, my family has always been religious in a customary way, mostly for show, but not spiritual. I was raised not to give that much credence until I experienced this connection through your talk." Tears came to her eyes. She paused and dabbed her eyes with a napkin. "I don't want to be a renunciate, as I believe they call nuns, but I want to deepen my connection to . . . whatever this is. I hope that isn't sacrilegious?"

"Mary, from what I've experienced, everything is sacred, and nothing is *oacceptabel*, as we Swedes say. Capisce?"

Mary nodded her head. "So let's just do a . . . deepening of this experience first, and then later, we can explore the other option."

Lexi scooted over next to her on the sofa and took her hand. "Just close your eyes and go with the flow."

After so many connections to the Source, Lexi just dissolved into its throbbing white light as if it were the heart of humanity. She could feel Mary's presence there but couldn't distinguish her. Then, she suddenly heard her cry in ecstasy, "Oh, my God."

Lexi came back to herself and her surroundings first. She sat there and watched Mary's entranced face glow with this unique form of luminosity. Finally, after five minutes, Mary opened her eyes and just stared ahead.

"Take your time coming back. Drink some water." Lexi poured her a glass from the pitcher on the table. Mary drank it down. Moments later, she turned to her.

"I've got to share this, so tell me, how does that work?"

"Generally, you picture a person you know and have had contact with, or look at a color photo of them, and send your energy to them." Mary looked unsure or puzzled. "Just take several deep breaths and breathe out while visualizing a white cord between the two of you. And you'll either show up in a kind of astral body, which we call a 'waking dream,' or in an actual dream if they accept the contact. If not, there won't be a connection, and nothing will happen."

"An astral projection, are you saying?" she asked tentatively.

"Or, if you prefer, during normal dreaming, but after several connections, the cords are in place, and you can link up telepathically."

"Oh, that would come in handy."

Mary nodded her head. "Okay, I will need you to walk me through that, but let's go to dinner first. I've reserved a private room at the Sheraton 360°. Call a friend or two, who can be discreet, and we'll all dine together. And afterward, you and I will come back here and . . . what do they call it, propagate this energy?" she asked.

"Okay, I'll call my lawyer Gretchen and her husband Didrik and my friends Anna and Liam, who are all initiated, and we can share our experiences with you."

"Good. Don't tell your friends who they're meeting, but my security people will take their phones. No pictures."

"They'll understand, and I bet you can entertain us with your own wild stories."

"Oh, yeah. The Royals are a bunch of cuckoos."

"I can well imagine."

24

San Francisco, California

While the advance copy of *Time* magazine with its cover story about "The Global Awakening" came to her office, Maria didn't have the time with her busy schedule to read it. As a prime contributor, she had already read the galley proofs to correct any mistakes in their reporting of her comments. Sitting on the patio of her Twin Peaks duplex and sipping a glass of Cabernet, she read the whole story with its colorful photos. She had to smile at the born-again black revivalist pictures of the women in their colorful outfits dancing and apparently "praising the Lord."

When the magazine first approached her, she was leery of contributing to this article, despite assurances by their senior editor, who claims to have had one of these "experiences," that it would be fair coverage. But Evelyn, prevented from contributing by British security, convinced Maria that she needed to set the record straight, or they might misrepresent this awakening. And while they interviewed Lexandra Berg because her speech was claimed by many to have initiated their contact with "God," Catherine flatly declined their invitation. She didn't want to be spotlighted as a "celebrity propagator," as she termed it.

What astonished Maria was the magazine's extensive investigative coverage around the world. They estimated that some two million people in the developed West alone claim to have already had these waking or nighttime dream "awakenings." And that number was increasing exponentially every day, especially among children. However, this number was still far below the 13 million, or one percent of the West's population, or 80 million worldwide, to spark de Chardin's Omega Point. Catherine's father, Barry, had told them that down through history, that was the magical percentage for any spiritual experience to get tripped into the general population, as he claimed. What would happen then was anybody's guess, but Western governments were undoubtedly concerned, not to mention China and India with their vast populations.

What was also impressive were interviews and semi-endorsements from such stellar world figures as Cardinal DiNapoli from the Vatican, Princess Tara and her royal family, and the U.S. Secretary of State Edwin Parker, among others. None were forthcoming when asked about the spread of these experiences to their families or associates. However, the Vatican's spokesman for this "global awakening," Reverend Dante Belmonte, said that his own "God" vision was moving, and he encouraged the faithful to consider this form of "renewal." This was the most unexpected major endorsement, although Maria wasn't surprised after their meeting with the emissary and his personal experience of the dreaming energy.

Maria's claim that some therapists, including Jesuit Dr. Mateo Russo, associated the Jungian concept of the Self, the organizing force here, with what most people considered as God sparked some disclaimers by other Jungian doctors interviewed. And while the CIA and MI5/6 were approached, if not the Russian SVR, none would give an interview about this "Black Swan" event, as most were now calling it. A so-called legitimate insider in the global security community spoke of their apprehension of a "viral spread" of these waking dreams in the general population, calling it a form of mass psychosis "like what overtook Germany in the 1930s." Other insiders disputed that claim.

Maria's phone chimed. She looked at the Caller's I.D. and answered it. "Hey, Cat, what did you think of the article?"

"The article? I'm surprised you're even taking calls."

"Only a few people have my private number, but at the office, Claire is swamped with calls for media interviews and new patient inquiries."

"Yeah, and unfortunately, me too. *Time* went ahead and kept me in the story, despite your objection. I might have to change my phone number."

"Any feedback?" Maria asked.

"I was really surprised by their two-million-dreamer estimate. So this outreach is moving pretty fast, and this article should speed it up."

"Yeah, and why the FBI/CIA pressured the magazine to can it."

Catherine sneered, "All those telepathic exchanges they can't listen in on. How dreadful for them." She paused. "Oh, speaking of that, Elena contacted me. Hers and Inna's family are safely tucked away somewhere."

"Good. What about the FSB woman, Galina?" Maria asked.

"We've both tried contacting her, but she's not accepting our tune-ins, as I guess you could call it."

"I'm sure she's hidden away too if she got this far working for the paranoid FSB," Maria said. She paused. "So this dreaming energy seems to have a life of its own and doesn't need much prodding by us any longer."

"Tell me, Lexi says she's getting calls from bigtime musicians and Hollywood filmmakers who want to know how to 'spread the energy.'"

"First, the musicians can turn down the volume," Maria said.

"Tell me." She paused. "Let's meet soon, either a dream contact, or we can have lunch somewhere private."

"Is that even possible now? I had someone at lunch yesterday ask me to sign their *Time* magazine." Maria thought about it. "How about another drive down the coast on Saturday to make up for our last misadventure there?"

"Sure. I love driving along the ocean, and we need a break from it all. So you bring Michael, and I'll bring Stephanie, and it'll be a real hoot."

"Yes, it will."

"Good. I'll pick the two of you up around 9:00, but we may have a follow car," Cat added.

"Okay. We'll talk ahead of time, but stop someplace for lunch and invite the guys in."

"Oh, yeah. Roy's even cute, but I don't know about Henry. Probably doesn't eat Mexican."

Maria laughed, clicked off, and sat back in her chair as the sunset and the twilight enveloped the city. It had been a crazy six months, but it felt like they had planted the seed, and it was time for everyone to nurture it. These waking dreams added a whole new dimension to her practice and added more ways for people to heal themselves. One doctor recently told her, "This is going to put us all out of business someday." Good. She needed a second career.

Moscow, Russia

When Galina came home from work in the middle of the day, her father, Fedor, knew something was wrong. As a former KGB agent, he could smell trouble on people, or that's what he used to claim. So when she went to the kitchen cabinet and took down a bottle of Vodka, he knew they were both in trouble. She poured each of them double shots. Fedor had enough sense to let his daughter tell her tale.

"Dad, do you still have, what do they call it, a 'go bag'?"

"Yes, with new passports and identity cards for both of us."

Galina was amazed. "Really."

"With my past and your present employer, and your moral conscience, as we talked about, I figured we might need to 'bug out of town' one of these days, as the British bad guys say on TV."

"Okay. I'm in trouble with FSB. I protected an asset by alerting her to an imminent capture, and she eluded them."

Fedor shook his head. "And you left a digital or phone trail?"

"I'm not that lame. There's a lot I haven't told you, Dad, and while what I did was undetectable by them, only I could do it."

He stared at his daughter. "Does this have something to do with how you've been lit up these days?"

"You can tell."

"Yeah, but we'll talk about that later." Fedor went back to his bedroom. She could hear a floorboard being pried loose. He came back with a passport and a package of red hair dye.

Galina opened the folder and saw her picture with red hair and a new name. "Yeah, I can do that color remake." She shook her head. "But how did you . . . oh, forget it. I'll dye my hair; you get us ready to 'bug out.'" She stopped walking away and turned back to him. "I assume we have someplace to go."

"You're going to love it. Nice little cottage on the Volga River south of Nizhny Novgorod."

Two hours later, they were heading east on the M7 four-lane highway. Her father had torn up and thrown away a map of western Russia with the M-11 route to Saint Petersburg marked. That escape route would make the most sense to the FSB agents. There, they could have snuck across the border to Finland or caught a boat to Sweden, sending their pursuers in the opposite direction. Moreover, they figured that this awakening would one day renew Russia's people, and they would rebel against their criminal political regime. They wanted to be here for that.

The used and somewhat battered Soviet-era Volga Galina was driving had been retrieved from a storage lot one metro stop farther east from their location. Her father bought the car years ago and maintained it for just such an escape. When he opened the storage lot's locked gate, removed the tarp covering the vehicle, and started it up, Galina was amazed. Her father had always been a great planner, but this foresight was eerie.

"How long has this been sitting here, Dad?"

Fedor was placing a new 2022 license plate on the back of the car. "Ten years or so. I take it out for a spin once a year, change the oil, gas it up, and use it for an occasional trip."

"You mean we could've been driving around in this instead of taking the metro for years."

"And it would've gotten on their radar." He pointed to the license plate. "In an old colleague's name. Untraceable to us."

Her father stood up, folded the tarp, and put it in the truck with their suitcases. Fedor handed his daughter the keys. "You drive. You've got better eyesight, and it'll get dark soon."

The 400-kilometer drive to Nizhny Novgorod took six hours in light traffic. Fedor slept for a couple of hours but woke up as they got closer. Outside of town, he had Galina pull into a roadside diner at a truck stop. The first thing she did was look around for CC cameras. Fedor laughed. "This isn't London or New York." There weren't any. They took a table in the back, away from the others.

After the waitress took their order and left, her father took out his battered brown leather wallet and handed Galina a credit card. It had her new name and was from a local bank. Again she looked at it in amazement. "You've been planning this for ages?"

"My first boss at the KGB once told me to start working out an escape plan after I was there for a few years. I assume he thought I might be doing something underhanded. But no, it was because I wasn't dirty, and the others resented that. The same goes for you. Given my KGB background, I knew that you'd get drafted into security work one day, so I began working out this plan for the same reason."

"You want to know what it's all about?"

Fedor shook his head. "Not here, but we'll have that talk when we get to the cabin."

Galina added, "Don't display your dirty laundry in public?"

Her father nodded his head.

After stopping in town for groceries, they backtracked to the M7 highway and headed south along the Volga River. At one point, they turned east to Mikhal'chikovo on the Nizhny Novgorod Oblast. They took a long dirt driveway to a cabin near the river without any neighbor's lights in sight. The electricity and gas were turned on. It was freezing, and it took a while for the furnace to warm the place. Otherwise, it was furnished with old furniture from the 1990s, but it appeared nicely maintained by somebody. Just a thin layer of dust everywhere.

"I pay a local woman, a pensioner, the widow of a friend from the old days, to keep it up. Don't worry. After what the state did to her husband, she'll keep quiet about us. And besides, we're kind of friends."

Galina looked at her father. "You know those little out-of-town trips I made over the years to visit . . . friends." He nodded. "She's a good cook, among other things."

"You should've told me, Dad. I'm glad you found somebody else after Mom died."

"You did take yearly lie detector tests." She understood. "Don't worry about Eva. She doesn't have family and isn't close to anybody here besides me. We're safe, or for now."

After the cabin had warmed up enough to take off their coats, they sat on the sofa. Galina told her father about what had been happening at work or her investigation of Elena and the others.

"So that's why they flew you to Moscow? You were pretty junior for that kind of trip. Figured it was something scientific but very specialized."

"Yes, Dad. But, after having this, I guess I can call it a dreaming experience; it changed everything for me."

"I was raised an atheist, but my work back in the 80s with psychic assets opened me to other possibilities." He paused. "And you can, as you say, pass it along?" Galina nodded. "There isn't much we can do here. There's a library in the back bedroom but no TV, or not yet. So I guess, for now, the inner journey is all that's left to us."

"Okay, Dad. Close your eyes and let me take your hand."

Soon his breathing had changed, his body relaxed, and Fedor Ilyin, the former KGB killer, was no longer an atheist.

25

Hong Kong, China

Within months, given her listeners' profound experiences, Bai Jin's radio talk show had become one of the most popular in China. Of course, her audience was aware enough not to discuss spiritual experiences over the air, given the censorship of such topics. But it was hard for the government to hold back the tide as other affected broadcasters on radio and television, none of whom were pressing an agenda, just beamed with a new light. With Madame Wang's political contacts on the mainland, Bai's boyfriend, Li Wu, had been monitoring any political backlash. With China's 1.4 billion population, hundreds of thousands of people getting "charged up" didn't seem to alarm the government. However, the *Time* article on the "Global Awakening," while banned on the mainland, precipitated an investigation by the MSS, The Ministry of State Security. They focused on enemy agents, spies, and counterrevolutionary activities that threatened China's socialist system—religious movements fell under the last category.

Through Wang's political network, Li had heard that the MSS had dispatched a high-ranking official to Moscow to consult with Russian security about these "waking dreams" and their propagation in Russia and the West. He returned to China alarmed enough to investigate "radio and television hosts" whose audiences displayed "unusual and provocative tendencies." They also scrubbed Lexandra Berg's speech from Hong Kong's Facebook feed. Finally, when one prominent newscaster was given an MRI that detected "a brain anomaly caused by a foreign contagion," Li knew it was time for Bai to come down with an illness and exit from her talk show gracefully. Hopefully, they could both get out of China before the hammer fell. But, of course, she did not see it that way at first.

While Bai and Li were careful about public appearances together, the well-paid staff at his high-rise condo building did look the other way when Bai came there on "official business." Tonight, Li cooked her favorite guilty-fare Cantonese dish, Shrimp Roe with long noodles, which looks like spaghetti with Marinara sauce. He served it with a delicate white wine. After dinner they sat on his Roma L-shaped white-leather sofa and looked out at Victoria Harbour.

Bai ran her hand over the smooth leather sofa arm. "You're buttering me up for something, Li?"

"Maybe I just want sex."

"That you can get any time, Hon. But something's on your mind. Remember, I can sense the currents."

"An MSS officer has come back from Moscow alerted to the propagation—I believe the Dumont woman calls it—of this dreaming energy over media broadcasts. They've already removed Berg's speech from Hong Kong's Facebook feed."

"The *Time's* article?"

"Yes, I believe that was the trigger. I mean, the Russians don't usually share such common threats with us communists. In their mind, we're growing too powerful, and their rich oligarchy fears a revival of socialism in their country."

"But, as Cat says, the West's research can't identify a carrier wave, so they wouldn't know who's spreading what."

Li nodded his head and took a sip of his wine. "Yes, but given that pilfered DARPA report she sent us, an MRI can spot the alterations in right-brain matter indicative of this energy's transmission."

"Damn. And the MSS will give suspected broadcasters brain scans?" Bai asked impatiently.

"They're conducting surveys to detect heightened responses among radio listeners and TV viewers from on-air exchanges with their hosts."

Bai sighed. "So it's only a matter of time?"

Lin nodded his head. "Yes, and that's why my family's doctor, paid to be discrete, will discover your brain tumor that needs immediate attention. I've talked with him, and he can arrange a bogus treatment for you at a prestigious cancer hospital in Melbourne, Australia, known for its holistic approach."

"Oh, and given my health regiment and diet, excluding tonight's meal, it would make more sense than Hong Kong's Adventist Hospital?"

"Exactly. While the Aussies are big trading partners with China, they're politically aligned with the U.S."

"And Dr. Amidala has connections at the White House who are open to this awakening."

"Yes, given that their Secretary of State is mentioned in the *Time* magazine article and talks about his dreaming experiences. So I think we'd be safe there."

Bai thought about this for a moment. "And if the MSS discovers that my listeners have been affected, I can claim it was the brain tumor affecting me, but I won't return until things change here."

"That's the plan. Also, I can leave my job with Wang, and my family has mining interests in Australia that I can manage. So we can sit it out there."

"Wow, Li. You've moved pretty quickly. I'm impressed. I think this calls for some great sex," she laughed.

But Li was still all-business. "And you agree to this masquerade?" Bai nodded. "Okay, you'll have to collapse during a radio broadcast. You can take a drug to create the kind of seizure most common with brain tumors."

"Won't the ambulance just take me to the nearest hospital?"

"Yes, but not for treatment. You'll start having symptoms tomorrow, and since Dr. Zheng is also a brain specialist, given my family history, you can first go to him for a checkup. After that, he'll falsify x-rays, and after your faked stroke, he'll intervene and have you flown to Australia."

Bai set down her glass of wine, rolled over, and straddled Li's lap. "Let's try something new. What Catherine calls dreaming sex."

"Lead on, my dear."

London, England

When the supervisors at MI5 discovered Gerald Harris, head of their Waking Dream Task Force, had leaked to SVR Officer Vlad Petrov a possible hiding place for the Russian dreamer Elena Mongush, they sent him into retirement. While Officer Davies had passed the information as ordered by his boss, he was absolved of any guilt and placed in charge of the task force. In the debrief with his superiors, Davies confessed that he had one of these waking dreams. But given that MI5/6 was now following the American lead from containment to management, they felt this exposure would be an asset. His first action was to mend the fence with Jungian analyst

Evelyn Richardson. He set up an appointment with the professor in her office at London University.

As Davies sat across from Evelyn and told her he was now in charge of the WD investigation, she sighed in relief.

"So they put that asshole Harris out to pasture?"

"With a distinguish service commendation for his work with Russian dissidents."

"And now MI5 wants to kiss and makeup?" Evelyn sniffed.

"Yes, I guess you could say, but what concerns me, and I would like your expert opinion on this concern, is as this dreaming energy pervades the world, how will the bad actors react?"

She chortled. "So someone there has half a brain, after all." She paused. "There are real forces of light and darkness in the universe. From my experience, they have to act through individuals, either lightbearers or compromised hosts in our world. So far as the psychology of bad actors, they are usually people who have lost something, or what gave them validation as a person, and which they project onto their country of origin. That's how wars start, not over disagreements or plays for resources, but people like Hitler trying to reclaim Germany's lost greatness. Sound familiar?"

"Someone like that comes to mind," Davies said. He paused. "Yes, and not just Russia. We expect China's president to make a move on Taiwan in the near future as well. Continuing what they started with Tibet."

"One of the early 20th-century's spiritual lights, the German mystic and philosopher Rudolph Steiner, identified the evil operating in Adolph Hitler from the beginning. In 1921, Steiner warned Europe against the disastrous effects if Hitler's National Socialists ever came to power in Germany. Some say Steiner's spiritual power kept that miscreant in check until he died in 1925."

"And as this light energy pervades the world?"

"It will be the only check to the power-hungry despots using their country's so-called manifest destiny to fill the holes in their psyches."

"And there's no hope for such warped people?" Ron asked.

"There's always hope since their core being is part of the same group Soul as everyone's." "That's good to know."

"So, Officer Davies, I hope you got what you came for."

"It appears you're telling us to promote and not suppress this awakening in people to offset the growing darkness." Evelyn nodded. "For which I agree."

After his meeting, Davies bundled up and strolled around the snow-covered campus as the students hurried from one heated classroom to the next. He could see the tension in their faces, the fear that their world would soon crumble and their education would be for naught. Ron wondered about his future and that of his world too. Finally, he went to a local tavern and student hangout. Davies sat down, ordered a London Pride ale, and watched the students viewing the news on the telly and debating the issues.

They were more relaxed here; the liquor probably helped. Ron recalled his student days at UOL and what he had hoped for himself. He would never have imagined going into British security as a career. Like the rest of the students, Ron had disparaged such a career choice back then. He had thought of teaching literature or philosophy but soon found that too dry and intellectual. Ron wanted to make a difference in people's lives and his country's welfare, but the military and city police forces were too regimented for him. It was why he got his Ph.D. in political science, which led him to the British Security forces.

While he had twelve years of Catholic education growing up, he was never religious in the traditional sense of that word. His Jesuit teachers were more philosophical than old-fashioned die-hards. But Ron had to agree with the basic precepts of his religion, and the sayings of Jesus Christ were more his bible than the Good Book. He wondered if that accounted for his ready acceptance of this dreaming energy.

Suddenly, a woman in her late twenties, red-haired with freck-les, pretty in a rumpled sort of way, sat down across from him in his booth. "Sorry to intrude on your bemused thinking."

"That obvious, is it?"

"In these haunts, yes." She smiled. "I'm Dorothy Stern, a teacher of sorts at the university."

"Of sorts?" he asked playfully. He liked the woman's looks and manner.

"Yeah, a multidiscipline pundit, as they call me."

"Hope you're not spread too thin these days."

"Actually, looking at situations, personal or international, from different angles adds stability, not chaos."

"I agree. The all-angle approach is my mainstay."

She nodded, then unexpectedly reached across the table and took his hand.

"If you're trying to pass me energy like they say these days, I've full to the brim," Ron said.

"I can see that. I was hoping you would share some with me."

"Oh, really," he said. Davies paused and looked more closely at the woman. "Okay, but first, you have to pass a test."

"Oh, goody. I like a challenge."

"It's a word puzzle: What's above us, around us, below us, and within all things?"

"Oh, that's easy: Light."

He now squeezed her hand. "Nice to meet you, Dorothy. I'm Ron Davies."

26

San Francisco, California

Maria was standing in the foyer of her Twin Peaks duplex, waiting for Michael to bring down their travel bag. She could hear the light tap of a car horn outside. *Pretty cheeky of Cat*, she thought.

"Come on, Michael. It's just a day trip."

He finally shuffled down the stairs with the small duffel bag. Maria shook her head and opened the door. When Cat spotted the bag, she pulled the trunk release, and the lid popped up. They came down the steps, and Michael laid the bag inside and closed the trunk.

Stephanie stepped out of the passenger's seat and pushed it forward for them to get into the backseat.

Maria slid in first. "We haven't met. I'm Michael, Maria's lesser half." He shook her hand.

"Stephanie. Cat's better half."

"Yeah, we'll see about that," Catherine sniped. They all laughed, got situated, and Cat drove off.

Maria looked behind them. "What about the follow car?"

"They gave me a break today. The Feds are downsizing their coverage of me. Thank God."

Michael looked at her, but she shook her head. Another time.

It was cloudy but cool on this first Saturday in February, and the Mustang's top was down, but everyone wore light sweaters. As usual, there was lots of San Fran traffic, even on weekends. This slowdown stifled the exchanges between them until they turned south onto Skyline Drive, with its spectacular ocean views giving them more personal space, or so it seemed.

Michael said, "Always love the transition from the city traffic to this calming scenery."

Cat added, "Yes, it's almost like the transition from our busy monkey mind into the inner sanctum." There was a long silence. "What? Did I break the mood?"

Everyone laughed. "You think," Stephanie finally said.

"Oh, so it's going to be that kind of day."

Maria mused, "Yeah, we all need a break from the inner sanctum."

"Speak for yourself," Michael quipped. She laughed at this late-comer to their "party."

Cat drove down from Skyline to the beach road. They passed Pacifica Beach, where there were few sunbathers on this cloudy day.

Stephanie asked, "Do you think it's too cool to go out and lie on the beach?"

"Maybe the sun will peek through," Maria added. "I hope you brought a one-piece, Stephanie; we don't want to get Michael too excited. I told him how the wind can blow off your bikini tops."

All the women laughed, having already decided on that. "Demure" was the ladies' word of the day.

"I'll try to restrain myself," Michael joked. Maria took his hand.

As they drove along the beach road, all were mesmerized by the ocean and the sandy beaches without the sun blazing overhead. Finally, the road turned inland at Mori Point for a two-mile stretch.

After a moment, Catherine sighed. "Wow. I needed this break. I mean, even work has gotten intense these days."

"I'm getting that vibe from my analysands, too," Maria blurted out, shaking her head.

"Tell me. My clients are so rattled by the world crisis that they're telling me to sell, sell, sell," Michael added.

Stephanie looked back at him over the center console. "You're a financial advisor?"

"Advisor, manager. I have private and corporate clients." He paused for a moment. "Not to break the mood, but I'm wondering if people will need my services in the . . . world to come."

Maria said, "A colleague was just telling me these self-healings will put psychiatrists out of business. So maybe we'll both need new jobs."

Cat looked at them in the rearview mirror. "Not anytime soon, I would imagine."

The road turned back to the ocean view for a mile or two and drew their attention. And then came the mile-long Devil Slide Tunnel with its glaring lights.

"Talk about dampening the mood," Michael exclaimed.

"This used to be a pretty dangerous stretch of road. I can remember driving it in the 90s and zigzagging around the fallen rocks," Maria said.

The car drove out of the tunnel into the glaring light of the day. Everyone rubbed their eyes. Maria added, "I imagine that's like the birth experience, coming out of the darkness into the OR's bright light. Sound familiar."

Catherine shook her head. "We just can't get off the subject, can we?"

Stephanie clapped her hands. "I, Queen Stephanie, declare a moratorium on such talk."

"Yes, Your Highness," Maria replied with a smirk.

The road ran along the ocean for the next four miles, and everybody just soaked up the vibe. Then, finally, they started to pass signs for the local beaches. Then at Moss Beach, the road turned inland to Half Moon Bay.

"I say we go into town and eat breakfast before we even think about hitting the beach," Cat queried.

No one objected, and so she continued driving. They came to the sign for Spanish Town.

"Well, we could always revisit the dinosaurs, Maria."

"I think we'll pass on that."

Michael looked over at her. "Oh, what happened after our dinosaur dream?"

Stephanie perked up. "What dinosaur dream?"

Catherine looked over at her. "I'll tell you later." In town they found what looked like a good breakfast place. Unfortunately, they hadn't spotted any restaurants with outdoor dining tables. Maybe too early in the year.

"I think I remember this place from way back when. Looks cozy enough," Maria said

They had a broad breakfast menu; everybody ordered, and their coffee was served. Then, after the waitress left, the two couples sat there and looked across the table at each other.

Finally, Cat spoke up, "It's amazing how this dreaming movement has so dominated our lives in the last six months." Stephanie glanced over at her. "If I may, Your Highness."

"A dispensation is granted."

Maria said, "I know what you mean. It kind of blurs the strict reality lines."

Cat added, "Tell me. I don't know when I'll get a call to dream-connect; I guess you could call it."

"Eventually, I think the two worlds, 3-D and the light-filled sanctum, will intermesh for more of us," Maria said.

Michael laughed. "Bring it on." She nodded her head and smiled at him.

Their breakfast was served, and they ate and tried to talk about everyday matters. They especially noted that the pace of life had slowed down despite the world crisis. Could this be attributed to the dreaming energy? Michael asked. Afterward, they all sat back and let their meals settle. Then, suddenly, Catherine closed her eyes. Maria reached over and took her hand; moments later, she came back.

"Something is going to happen in Eastern Europe." She looked Maria in the eyes. "Guess we're *all* coming back to your place tonight."

"All?" Maria asked tentatively.

"I mean, all of us."

Michael waved for the check. "My treat while I still have clients."

The waitress came over, and he handed her his American Express. Then, he turned to the others. "I guess the beach outing is off, but we can still drive further south and take in the ocean vista before crossing over to 280 and heading back." They all agreed.

Catherine added, "I think 'crossing over' is the theme of the day."

THEY HAD CLEARED or pushed back Maria's living room furniture to create a wide circle with scented white candles. The four of them sat cross-legged on cushions with their eyes closed. Of course, they didn't need the physical space for the dreaming bodies to assemble, but psychologically it gave the placeholders, as they were called, a feeling of spaciousness. Although their minds were stilled, this get-together wasn't a group meditation; the four of them were more like the grounding poles of a vast electrical storm or vortex spread worldwide.

As its principal proponent, Catherine sent out the call into the ethers that summoned those who were available and willing to gather—friends, associates, dreaming connections, even those who had just awakened. But this caller was answering another call from the throbbing heart of humanity impinged by the growing darkness that could create more chaos and separation among the members of its human community—or depending on humanity's response. From the beginning, Cat could sense that, unlike previous vortex gatherings, this was less of a spiritual get-together of the awakened than, if not a call to arms, a call to action. This faceoff was not to fight or curtail but to integrate those driven unconsciously by the dark forces of the universe. Yes, while humanity was being tested, it was not just driven by the good and bad actors here but was a fight on this turf of a longstanding battle that spanned time and space.

As the call was answered, she could recognize those assembling: Evelyn Richardson, Fathers Belmonte and Russo, Secretary Parker, Lexandra and Princess Tara, Elena, Inna and David, Alicia and Greg, Galina and Fedor, Ron, Vlad Petrov, Kostya, and Arina Dorzhiev, General Morton, Barry and Joyce, Bai and Li, Andrew and Mickalene, and all those connected to them. Their energies added to the vortex's flow that grew wider and wider, encompassing the city, the state, and eventually the whole world. Those ready only needed to touch this energy bubble to be awakened as it permeated everything. Those who resisted just went about their night or daytime voyages.

The four gathered here lost awareness of the hour. When the vortex dissipated and those summoned returned home, as it were, the four placeholders opened their eyes. It was two o'clock in the morning. Maria retrieved bottles of water from the fridge and passed them out. Afterward, they all lay back, like with the Savasana pose in yoga, letting the energy integrate.

Finally, after a long while, Michael popped up. "I don't know about the rest of you, but I'm starving. How about pancakes? I know a great all-night eatery that serves all kinds of them."

The others sat up. Maria looked around at them. "You're on, Big Boy. Lead the way."

Michael drove his car with Maria, and Cat followed in her Mustang with Stephanie as they went down the hill, then across town to the restaurant on the east side. It was opened as advertised with several late-night diners. They took a table in the corner and ordered their pancakes and waffles.

After the waitress took their order, Catherine turned to her friends. "I hope that wasn't too much for anybody." They all looked a bit beleaguered but smiled.

Maria added, "But let's not do that again or anytime soon."

Catherine lifted her coffee cup. "Hopefully, humanity will soon dream up a better world for all of us."

They all clinked their coffee cups. "Let's hope" was the universal reply.

That night Maria and Michael saw the "green flash" from her patio.

The Beginning

About the Author

John Nelson is the author of the novels *Starborn*, *Transformations*, and *Matrix of the Gods,* initially published by Hampton Roads Publishing; and *I, Human*, published by Cosmic Egg; *The Miracle of Anna* by Roundfire books; *New Mexican Standoff* and its sequel, *The Serpent of Time*; and his Zen poetry book, *This Moment Paradise* were published by Bookworks Publishing. In addition, he authored the nonfiction book *The Magic Mirror*, published by HRPC, which won the 2008 COVR Award as the best book of the year and best divination system, and more recently, *A Guide of Energetic Healing* and *The Singularity of Consciousness.*

He was the editorial director of Bear & Company in the mid-1990s and Inner Ocean Publishing in the early 2000s. He has been the owner of Bookworks Ltd. since 2003, where he edits fiction and nonfiction books for various authors and publishers. This list includes *The Sacred Promise* by Gary Schwartz, *The 12-Step Buddhist*, *Yoga and the Twelve-Step Path*, *The Riddle of the Sphinx* by Alexandre Montagu, *Brainstormed* by Vladimir Lange, *Bright Light* by Dee Wallace, and *Luminous Living* by Jacob Liberman.

Nelson has been a yogi and a meditator for fifty years and brings an expanded consciousness perspective to all he writes. His fiction is usually a blend of hard science, science fiction, and psycho-spiritual insights.

Visit his website at www.johnnelsonbookworks.com.

Made in the USA
Middletown, DE
12 February 2023

23818402R00154